All the best,
Richard
May 15, 2014

≫ FOURTEEN ≪
SHORT STORIES

by

Richard Alan Bunch

∞INFINITY
PUBLISHING

Copyright © 2013 by Richard Alan Bunch

ISBN 978-0-7414-9849-6

Printed in the United States of America

Published September 2013

INFINITY PUBLISHING
1094 New DeHaven Street, Suite 100
West Conshohocken, PA 19428-2713
Toll-free (877) BUY BOOK
Local Phone (610) 941-9999
Fax (610) 941-9959
Info@buybooksontheweb.com
www.buybooksontheweb.com

To the memory of my parents

and to

Rita, Katie, and Rick

Grateful acknowledgement is made to the following editors and publishers in whose publications, earlier or final versions of these stories first appeared: *The Plaza, Language and Culture Review, Writers of the Purple Sage,* and *Goose River Anthologies.*

i

Table of Contents

Kismet

Whenever you would enter the large wall-filled library of Mr. Kismet, you would come out with the feeling of having seen a lifetime in only a few moments. It was like any other room I guess except that there pervaded in it a strangeness, a peculiar romance about it, that made it somehow different. The walls on the left were dotted with diplomas, certificates of all kinds conferring upon Mr. Kismet a sense of belonging, a sense of dignity that belonged solely to him. Somehow everything he associated with came out to grasp you and shake you out of the cornerstones of reality in favor of leisurely pipedreams.

With his hair graying about the temples, his eyes a merry and arrogant black, his jowls sagging slightly with age, Mr. Kismet cut a fine elderly picture. Out of the fog-enshrouded Jersey city of Princeton, he had shipped off to the German front in the first World War, all the while when behind the lines secretly courting the fairest frauleins imaginable, spending silent nights along the moon-swept waters of the slow-moving Rhine.

What fascinated me about his little cubbyhole of a room was that the very walls themselves seemed to whisper secrets of his past, a past more fascinating than fiction could muster the courage and audacity to spit out onto the printed page.

His son was my age and every day, through all the years of our acquaintance, he would take me into that room as if urging, quietly and subtly urging me, to put it into the inky markings of my prose.

No college degree supported him and I do not think Mr. Kismet gave a damn. He had come out of the stuffy high-class Princeton area with his family either having gone to Princeton or Rutgers through the last couple of generations. He had seen enough of all that.

I remember how we would watch him sitting there by the crackling fire and his eyes would look so sad, his head tilting over with sleep as if tired from doing a daily project that kept our imaginations alive with inquiry, to ourselves, of course. Every New Years that fire would burn like a lost youth in his eyes, his wife Oona sitting there with a highball in her hands, and spilling out gab that would make the Blarney Stone blush. But she danced, her eyes did, the fire crackled and popped and then midnight would strike and we would sing "Auld Lang Syne" with bravado, the ice in the glasses clinking as our arms waved high on the air.

Always after the party was over, and the gossiping, Mr. Kismet would depart for bed, his wife following easily and sleepily, leaving me with his son with whom I played hearts and black jack late into the dawn hours. The room stood there almost inviting us with its long arms of the past bidding us to come but with a dash of aloofness that urged us in. Every type of book conceivable for a literary mind lined his shelves: mysteries, science fiction, poetry, dramas, novels, stories of all kinds beckoned an avid reader to open their covers and partake of the print over which Mr. Kismet's eyes had swept.

Tucked within each book were mementoes and dates from 1909 to the stock market crash of 1929. Pictures of his first wife, Halfrida, were glued in the back cover, the one he had married after coming back to the states from the front. New Orleans, the "Big Easy," was his first stop. He adored the Latin Quarter; it reminded him so much of Paris. And how could you not love Paris?

While in Mississippi, he had met and talked with "Count No-Account," the nickname for the young William Faulkner. He also courted two Ole Miss coeds who are married to Memphis physicians to this day.

Halfrida was a partner in business with him but it did not last and so they split and he wandered, through Kansas City, the Ozarks of Missouri, the flat land around Detroit, the wavy fields of Nebraska, through the salt-saturated lake of Utah and through the desert interlude of Nevada and settled in the San Francisco Bay Area. It was in San Francisco that he painted huge yellow and red canvases, wrote his poetry for an anthology of forty-four California poets and married Oona from Pleasant Hill.

I remember his son asking him one evening how he liked the literature and poetry he had written.

"It's fine, I guess. Too damn much trouble pouring out your life on it though. I'd rather read the authors already on the market, the established ones like Carl Sandburg, Robinson Jeffers, Jack London, F. Scott Fitzgerald, Norris and the rest.

"Dad, did you ever write anything but poetry?" asked his freckle-faced son.

"A story here and there. It wasn't worth much. Too little time and I needed the money," he said, nodding all the while.

Mr. Kismet was a classy, well-mannered gentleman, dark, handsome and elderly. But very soon he died of a heart attack and he was buried on a sweet-scented grassy slope overlooked by hanging willow trees.

We cleaned up his room, and while putting his books in order we came across a burnished manuscript, its pages yellowish-brown from age. Dusting it off, we tried to make out the writing, scratched in black ink and labeled 1931. It was the torn fragments of a novel set on the German front with the 2nd Division of the United States forces at the battle of Chateau-Thierry when the German advance was broken. It was entirely autobiographical; his thoughts and sentiments about war and about life. It told of his being brought up in a middle class neighborhood in New Jersey, his conflicts with his father, his wanderings all over the continent, his enlistment in the service and his round about journey to California. Perhaps the most impressive portion of the manuscript was about the war, the futile days and nights when, at any moment, he could be shot and left a bloody carcass in a trench or foxhole. But in the margin he left a special message; in a different color of ink; not faded like the others in the manuscript as if he had written it only days before his death. It read: "After life, war is hell. When all the sweet dawns and sunsets have departed, 'tis sweetest in death; then you only wage war with your soul."

We looked baffled at one another, the manuscript spread on his desk. When we went up the grassy slope to put roses on his grave the following Saturday, the ground looked as though it had been ground up, the dirt spread out like a fan. Apparently the gravestone had been moved. Lying in a clump of moist earth ten feet away from the burial site was an exact facsimile of that novel manuscript, the torn pages flipping this way and that way in the wind.

Our eyes, we thought, were deceiving us. Someone had marked the gravestone. It had his name Orville Kismet, dates 1891-1957, and then mysteriously it read: "suffering is the way of the world."

We put the roses gently on the grave and walked away, both of us, turning at every few steps to see the novel flapping in the wind and the flowers blowing this way. How the novel got there, no one knew. Or would ever know.

Veiled Interlude

Outside the pub, fog continued to further diminish the faint glow of the darkening sun. Inside, Wendy waited on some gents dressed in gray, brown, and blue Scottish tweeds, their faces ruddy, their talk a quiet hum. Methodically, she poured tall glasses of lager, ale, and stout until thick foam formed at the top. Though her brown eyes were calm, she had a faintly mischievous smile. Handsome in his army uniform, or so his mother once said, Aaron sat there and could not take his eyes off of her. He had done this before, although he was not becoming a nuisance about it. He simply liked her and their conversations on previous nights. The night before he decided she was for him; he liked her lips—the way they formed an alluring heart-shape—not to mention her straight black hair and that hint of Britannia in her demeanor that on these blackout nights possessed a touching warmth.

She came over and smiled for she recognized him as one of the Yanks she had met nights before and the one man she liked having a conversation with. The Yanks were stationed here to help fight the Nazi menace that could still use its control of northern France to threaten this little island "set in the silver sea." They had a spirited conversation the night before and when, in a moment of loneliness and near despair, he had asked her to have a drink with him after work. She did.

"Let's see if I remember," she teased Aaron, "Macheson Stout?"

"...and two ham rolls," he added.

"You will have them," she replied, smiling as she left. He watched as she passed behind the walnut brown bar and pulled down a thick, dark bottle. Into a pint glass she poured the thick ale. Coolly, Aaron stared at her as though she was a deer about to sprint into a virgin forest. Several customers stood at the bar; others talked quietly, as they sipped pints of bitter. She circled and wove her way through them and brought him his drink.

"Here we are," she said. "Your rolls will be a few minutes."

He beckoned her to come closer.

"Can I see you later tonight?"

She thought a moment and nodded with a smile. This young man appealed to her, in part because he was American and thus different from other blokes in this part of England but also, in part, because he was a stranger, someone she could get wild with. No one knew him. His anonymity allowed him liberties with her and, her with him, that she would seldom allow the local blokes. And Aaron was not one to avoid a wild time where he could find it. After all, he was from the States. And he had to do so within the limits of curfew and blackouts. Other limits were too long to list: everything could only be measured in time: how he had left his proud but sad parents in Bayonne; induction into the army; having to wear a uniform at all limited him, he thought. Time and time again he was tempted to go, just leave, to desert, but an ample streak of patriotism tempered such thoughts which were now interrupted as she set two ham rolls on his table.

"I've asked him," she said, gesturing in the direction of the bartender who was drying some pint-sized glasses, "and he says I can go since we close early anyway. I don't want to stay here and drink, Aaron," she added with a curious mixture of pleading and exotic forbiddenness in her voice.

He had finished one roll and was biting into the second one, when Wendy emerged from behind the bar with her coat in hand. She was ready to go. He rose and took her hand as they ventured into the foggy night. Salty coastal breezes pervaded the night air. They made their way down side streets until they reached the edge of town.

"I brought it for us," she said, pulling a candle from her coat pocket.

This caught Aaron by surprise. What did she have in mind? he thought. On they strolled until they came to what looked like it was at one time an alehouse. Wendy assured him she was familiar with it and, taking him by the hand, she led him in. As far as they knew, no one had seen them go in. Darkness enveloped them. A scent of wood and hay emerged in one corner of the structure as the tiny flicker of the candle endowed it with a faint pinkish glow.

"God, you're bold," he said as she grinned broadly.

"I do like some Yanks, especially someone I know." Wendy had seemed somewhat shy before and now she was coming on so strong it almost scared him. She unbuttoned his coat as his heart raced. Aaron was bowled over by her audacity. Her legs felt warm next to his, though her fingertips were cold. After awhile as the loving subsided, she became serious with an almost wistful look on her face.

"You're so young...such a fine man...why another war?" she said.

"There has to be another war because...people love it. Or they're bored and want to be important..." he mused absently even though it was obvious he was becoming annoyed by the insertion of war into their conversation. Though she noticed the disgust in his voice, amazingly she continued:

"When do you have to go?"

"Not too long. I can't talk about it. Not now."

"I will miss you," she said, stroking his jaw line. He smiled pensively but said nothing. The glow of the candle grew more and more faint. At least if it were to go out, they knew where they were in the room. They knew where the door was. Wind now and then whirred through cracks in the wood and stone and an occasional gust spun bits of hay around on the floor. Still this old place was a relief against the night. They kissed again long and longer.

Outside, the fog harbored the military might and determination of those whose turn it was to answer the call to join in the praise of folly. Wars were easy to start: border disputes, trampling ambition, uncreative boredom, insults real or imagined, testosterone overload, purist bigotries, prolonged amnesia, religious fanaticism, visionless glory, power seductions, imperial arrogance, will contests, and the list went on. Yet it was peace that was hard. Waging peace was the most difficult to master since it included mastering hatred, ego, and ignorance. In the distance, in the shell fire night of sea breezes and the muted drone of planes could be heard high above clouds embellished by thick covers of fog.

Their brief time slipped away like birds dissolving in flight. As the wind increased, a window pane rattled like soft tapping fingers in the night. Their candle formed glowing pools at its base, pools that would soon strangle the now-diminishing flame. He stared as the flame's reflection danced on her smooth flesh.

After a long time, he said:

"The candle's going out."

"Don't worry. We can find our way in the dark."

"Still. We had better go. I've got to get back. Besides, you don't have another light."

Reluctantly, very reluctantly, she acknowledged that fact. They zipped and buttoned up and made their way out into the darkness. The wind blew her hair across her face which was still wistful and a little sad.

It was not far to her house; they kissed long on the porch stairs. He told her he would see her again tomorrow night. After such an assurance, and a touching evening, however crude or modest, she went inside. Although he desperately wanted to, he knew he could not see her again. There were too many things to do and think about. Besides, he could not take saying goodbye. It was better this way, he thought. It was only a matter of hours until he would be going to France. He would get to know Omaha Beach intimately in the pivotal invasion of Normandy. He would never see her again. But now, as he rode back to the base, he could barely hear the faint hum of high-altitude planes and distant bombardment. He also knew, in the sea breezes of this war, an armada of fog-enshrouded ships lay ponderous, poised and ready on the restless and brooding Channel. It seemed as though this would be the twilight of the gods.

In spite of this, maybe tomorrow will be sunny, he thought, yes, tomorrow.

The One Hundred Club

Erehwon Manor, once a family residence, rises out of gray morning mists like an ocean liner looms out of a thick fog at sea. Architecturally, it is a masterpiece of Elizabethan and Jacobean design with the excessive ornamentation of the Victorian era in which it was built. It is also the scene of a biannual hunt of the One Hundred Club which provides hunting opportunities for those who have to be at least one hundred years old.

On a Sunday in December and June, they meet in town and drive out to Erehwon with their shotguns and boxes of shells to shoot pheasant. Trees, shrubs, uncut weeds and grasses and hedges of various heights surround the manor. A swamp that was at one time a lake broods on the west side of the property with a statue of a missionary praying in front of it. There is also rumored to be a fountain of youth somewhere on the manor property. When one drinks of its waters, one ceases to get old, becomes healed, and can see at the bottom of the fountain the sacredness of water as portrayed in so many religions and folk tales all the way back to the Rig Veda of ancient India. But none of the hunters has so far found it. Or if one has found it, not one word has been said about it or its restorative properties.

I parked my car in the enclosed bull ring at the front of the manor. As I walked up the steps leading to the cricket field, I began to see some hunters at various parts of the manor grounds. One hunter in gray boots and Sherlock Holmes hat, clomped through some tall weeds at moments stalking as though he heard something about to flush out of the weeds, at others standing up as though listening to the cooing of pigeons in the trees. At one point, I stood behind a tall shrub at the top of the lawn that sloped down to the cricket field below only to be startled by an older man with slumped shoulders and grayish hair and slight sideburn curls, bowed low and said to my surprise: "Dr. Livingstone, I presume." I assured him I was not the famed missionary and explorer. He bowed low as though to beg my pardon and soon disappeared into a nearby thicket. It was not long before I encountered an auburn-haired man with hunting cap and ruddy face who strutted out from behind a tall pillar. "Glad I checked first. Before I fired. I thought you was a pheasant."

"Do I look like a bird?" I said with unfeigned disgust.

"Come to think of it...you don't. Many pardons, Ma'am," he said as he disappeared into a grove of trees and thick underbrush.

To say that I was becoming disgusted, not to mention apprehensive, would be a vast understatement. So far, I had been mistaken for a missionary, a pheasant and even a woman. It did not seem this brief afternoon would be all that pleasant, even if I *were* a pheasant.

I had not proceeded more than twenty-five paces when an old gentleman dressed in blue trousers, gray knit sweater, and checkered cap stepped in front of me. He wore a black patch over one eye. He stooped over and his hands trembled and slightly shook while holding his shotgun that I figured must have weighed two or three pounds.

"S---s---Sonny. P----pardon me, but can you t--tell me where some pheasant are?" He tried to smile, but having only a few teeth, kept his lips closed most of the time.

"They're probably in those woods or out there in the fields," I said, indicating the long, newly-plowed, clod-knotted fields that stretched past the manor gate near a stream that ran under that part of the road that led to the manor.

"I s--see. Thankee Sonny," he said as he suddenly lifted the shotgun to his shoulder and swung the barrel across the horizon and fired. A large pheasant had got away with its life but the praying hands had not. They were chipped, causing some pieces to fall off, and the missionary's nose had been nicked. I decided to tiptoe away while he was looking the other way.

Although I made my way through low-hanging brambles to the statue of the watchful lion that slept at the back of the manor, a bullet zinged by my head. Then another. What to do? The shots stopped.

"You k---k---know somethin, s--s--sonny, I thought you was a lion." Then he laughed hard as though the whole world was laughing with him.

"No, I'm not a lion. You should be more careful. Open your eyes next time."

I left him and kept looking back as I moved away. I did not want to be shot at again. Next to a ramp leading to the back of the manor stood an elderly gent with a head of wavy white hair who looked almost young compared to some of the hunters I had already encountered. It turned out this bloke, whose name was Owyn Benflower, knew most of the hunters who regularly attended these hunting expeditions. He seemed much younger, a relative youngster in this crew. He held his gun pointed downward so it would not harm anyone.

"Who was that?" I asked.

"Oh, that was Nick. He gets a bit wild with a gun in his hands. We have to keep an eye on him."

"I'll say. He almost hit me in the head," I said matter of factly.

"He does get carried away..." Owyn said.

"Around these parts, he goes by the nickname 'Nick the One-Eyed Gunner'"

"Because he has a patch over one eye?"

"Well, he *is* blind in one eye. And should be wearing his glasses for the other."

"Oh, that should improve his marksmanship," I said somewhat sarcastically.

Just then Nick the One-Eyed Gunner began to amble in our direction.

"Here he comes again," I said to Owyn.

"Hey, Nick, take it easy. You scared my friend Jack Russell here. Your bullets nearly hit him. He ducked out of the way, you might say, in the nick of time."

After a low chuckle, Nick said: "S---s----sorry Sonny. So s---s---sorry."

"You need to be after the pheasants. That's what you came here for, Nick. They are probably over past that lawn near the woods," said Owyn, indicating a westerly direction past the cricket field and the elaborately carved tool shed.

"Thankee, Owyn. That you, Owyn?" he said, squinting, as though all he needed in the world was to focus more clearly.

"Yes, it's me, Nick. It's me." Nick gave us both a feeble salute then ambled off, holding his gun across his chest, ostensibly in pursuit of wild pheasant.

"Have a good hunt, Nick," said Owyn.

"How can somebody who's a hundred years old be allowed to hunt?"

"Hey, I'm a hundred and two."

"You are *not*. I don't believe it. You don't look a day over ninety-five." I said.

"I really am. Nick's a hundred and eight."

"Only six years older? He seems much older than you."

"People age at different speeds. They really do."

"You're very clear. You speak well. He can hardly speak clearly."

"Still, it's true. I may be just like that in six years," he said, sad at the thought.

After a pause, he continued:

"But back to your original question. It's a kind of recreation for senior citizens."

"But it's not recreation to be shot at!"

"That's true. This must be your first time."

"No, my second," I said with a measure of disgust.

"You might say it's a kind of occupational therapy," Owyn continued.

"Hmmmph," I grumbled. "Too many things are done in the name of therapy these days," I said.

"We all need a little therapy now and again," remarked Owyn as he continued to scan the manor grounds for other hunters. At most there seemed to be no more than seven hunters in all, one more than the last hunt six months earlier. After a few moments my curiosity got the better of me and finally I asked:

"How *do* you stay so young? You don't look very old at all. Certainly when compared to these other hunters here."

"I'm a retired archaeologist. Taught for over forty years at the local college. Still go on digs for bones, artifacts like jewelry, and bones now and then. But for the most part I'm just enjoying retirement."

"But how *do* you stay so young? And look so young at a hundred and two?"

Owyn thought a moment. Then he surveyed the manor grounds again.

"Well, it's easy to look young when you're surrounded by fossils," he said with a slight smile.

I had to agree. He looked at least ten to fourteen years younger than these hunters out here, especially Nick the One-Eyed Gunner. He discerned from my face that my curiosity had not been satisfied so he continued:

"No, I just stay active. Keep up with the latest fossil finds. And tend to my garden of roses and tulips. Keep them well tended. Go to the Blue Rhino, a pub near where I live. Play a few round of darts with the youngsters. Down some cool brown ale like Macheson Stout or Newcastle-on-Tyne. So it's not just to be around fossils since I am becoming one myself. But to eat some really fine food. That's one of the reasons I come to these hunts."

"Really. That's why I came today. Not to hunt but to have some of that delicious pheasant. Why last time I was here the cook, I think his name is Skip, made a roast pheasant with bacon and garlic that was scrumptious."

"He puts it together, doesn't he? And Shepherd's Pie, especially when he puts a layer of corn between the meat and potato layers with a dash of barbecue sauce. Deeelicious!" crooned Owyn.

"Whether it's beef or lamb curry. Or a salad with potatoes and beetroot with goats cheese, Skip's dishes make you forget you're here for the roast pheasant."

"And don't forget," added Owyn with gusto, "his famous dessert. Custard Pie."

"You're making me hungry," I said.

"And for another dessert, maybe in our spare time, we can look for a fountain of youth that's supposed to be on the property here somewhere but I haven't found it."

"I haven't either. That would be a baptism worth dying for," I said.

"We'll have to keep hunting won't we?"

"Indeed. We sure will."

Just then a flock of pigeons that had burst out from some thick trees were greeted with gunfire. Only one was shot down. Nick's gun had done the deed. Owyn shot his gun into the air to get Nick's attention.

"Hey, Nick! Hey, Nick!" Nick looked over in his direction.

"Did that look like a pheasant?" Reluctantly, Nick shook his head.

"Don't shoot the pigeons, Nick. We're here for pheasant. Remember that."

At that point, I decided to stay inside the manor; it appeared to be too dangerous to be outside with such hunters.

"I think I'll stay in the manor. There's some books in the library."

I understand. I should stay out here and keep an eye on these guys. You never know what might happen."

"You can say that again," I said as I walked through the large doors leading to the library with its collections of Mutswairo, Shakespeare, Transtromer, Unamuno, Woolf, Swinburne, Arrabal, Goethe, Wordsworth, Pirandello, Lao Tzu, Dostoevsky, Borges, and Keats, movies, TV series and concerts. In a couple hours, the hunt would be over. And the grand feast, well worth waiting for, would begin.

Meditation Interruptus

Stapled to a tree trunk was a hand-painted sign announcing a performance of the music of India and meditational exercises led by prolific author and Zen devotee, Bhaghwan Mysore.

The three stood there reading it.

"We should go," Mark said.

"Yes, let's. I like Mysore anyway," declared Orestes.

Sandy just smiled in her usual bemused way.

The Saturday following they arrived at the university campus and parked near tennis courts as reddish-hued as the clay of north Georgia.

"That's the beauty of the full-lotus position," concluded Mark, "it's the balance and low center of gravity..."

"How do you know so much about it?" asked Orestes.

"Years of practice. And much reading."

Mark was almost boastful about his buoyant interest in Buddhist meditational techniques. He had developed his interest in meditation about four years earlier due to the influence of a friend of his father who was a member of the White Robed Monks of St. Benedict, an order of Dutch Catholic monks that practice Zen sitting or zazen. A student at the university, he was majoring in philosophy and art; his extensive meditational experience had disciplined his mind and made him, so he said, a calmer person. His shoulder-length dark hair floated over his Hawaiian shirt that featured the entire island chain and fluttered slightly in the breeze as he described his favorite subject. Sandy listened carefully; she respected Mark's opinion; for her, this was an area she knew nothing about but was interested in, especially since she had begun dating Orestes.

"The idea is to calm the mind by calming your samsaric thoughts; that is, your everyday thoughts are distractions that prevent you from focusing your life, your being," explained Mark.

"But how do you do that?" asked Orestes.

"Breathing. Focus on breathing...and the point where your nose becomes the focal point where you breathe in and out...You just concentrate your breathing and avoid outside distractions. I think you got the hang of it when we tried it last night. You both were able to shut out the sirens and other sounds of the night. You both did well. You didn't even need ear plugs. That's how some on this odyssey try it."

They passed an S-shaped pond where ducks and geese swam at leisure. An island, shaded by willows weeping, was connected to the land by a redwood arched bridge so people could pass over it and visit the little island where the ducks and geese slept at night. Passing an ivy-covered wall, they came to a large gymnasium where this festival of Indian music and meditation was to take place. They sat down toward the back near a scoreboard. Mats had been placed on the floor to alleviate cramping and discomfort that frequently accompanied sitting in meditational positions. Erotically exotic music by the group called *The Five Skandas* curled like smoke through the rafters: it included the twang of the sitar with its subtle, sensuous vibrations; castanets clicking; and bongo drums with a steady patter of rhythmic fingers calloused by years of playing.

At length, Mysore emerged and sat on a huge pink pillow; he then assumed the full-lotus position. His beard was streaked with silver. His pants were made of silk and fit rather loosely; his shirt billowed at the shoulders yet fitted snug about his wrists. The lights began to dim slowly. His aura remotely resembled that of a maharaja but his simple mode of being resembled that of a Zen monk. Greeting this large audience, he welcomed them to this festival of lights. About three feet in front of Mark and company was a blond girl seated in the full-lotus position with her purse, sweater, and bag of granola cereal next to her. Just at an angle to her was a door that remained ajar for latecomers. Mark assumed the full-lotus position, his thumb and index finger of each hand touching. His breathing deepened; he firmed his spine at a right angle to the floor, and neatly tucked each leg beneath his body for the full effect of a low center of gravity. The night before he had explained the touching of the thumb to the index finger as a symbol of cosmic unity. At times he would raise his hand with his index finger pointed up; he had explained that was gesture of peace of would-be

16

buddhas with all sentient beings. Sandy and Orestes watched him and they, too, assumed the full-lotus position. Sandy was much more used to this position, having tried it more times than had Orestes. But there he was—his blue-trimmed sweatshirt outlining large freckled muscular arms, his Levi's somewhat loose about the waist, his hair a bit shorter and browner than Mark's, his brown eyes adjusting to the subdued light—a portrait of an eager learner in this intoxicating mixture of body-space and time.

The entire gym was soon filled with meditation; the music became softer and more subdued until it finally ceased. Seated in the full-lotus position, Mysore lifted his hand in a gesture of peace, fingers pointed heavenward, his head still, his eyes half-closed, his spine erect, his breathing deep, and began to hum the sacred mantric syllable "OM", itself a symbol of unity, a symbol of harmony of the inner self with the cosmos, a perfect nasal-producing circle. It spread like ripples to the lips of everyone.

A sense of harmony through repeated versions of Ommmmmm Ommmmmm Ommmmmm Ommmmmm Ommmmmmmmmmm began to pervade the entire gym. Unity began to vibrate from their delicious breathing in this search for the experience of oneness, of the possibility of nirvana itself. As Mark had described to them the previous evening, the deeper the meditation the more relaxed brain activity would become until an indescribable sense of peace permeated one's being.

In his own way, Orestes was becoming quite relaxed, although his legs were beginning to feel uncomfortable. Though seated in the full-lotus position, Sandy also felt some discomfort. Both were glad mats had been provided. A deeper sense of relaxation and harmony began to be felt, as though global harmony were indeed possible, as though a sense of planetary peace were deservedly inevitable.

As mentioned, the door to their right and ahead of them had been left ajar. The angle of outside light, whenever the door was opened, fell right on the blond girl—affectionately dubbed Miss Om—who sat within a few feet of the door. Although some latecomers had used the door already, they had not disturbed this congregation of cosmic unity-producing devotees, this sea of cosmic vibrations, whose meditations on "Om" would produce a peace that passeth all understanding.

Sandy had noticed the German Shepherd whose name, as it turned out, was "Bam" —short for Bamboozle—as he frolicked among the meditators toward where Mysore sat aglow, it seemed, with the relentless rhythm of repeated Ommmmmmmmm Ommmmmmmmm Ommmmmmmmm Ommmmmmm that pervaded the gym. Bam was not one to meditate; in fact, Bam had much more mundane concerns on his canine mind. Far from any feelings of cosmic unity, Bam it seems was emphatically more interested in playtime.

Bam's thoughts, in this fair blossom time, had turned to a kind of lusty playfulness very much in that fashion of divine madness inspiring the animal world, including, of course, that sea of vibrations in which he was now sniffing about.

To this day neither Sandy, Orestes, nor Mark understood what it was about Miss Om's purse that attracted Bam. Perhaps her perfume: it was alarmingly alluring. Maybe it was the purse's soft leather. In any case, Bam got it into his head that Miss Om's purse was something he wanted to play with—and keep.

Once Bam perceived Miss Om's purse in this light, however unsavory it might appear, there was no delay. Bam wanted to frolic. Desperately so. And, after a routine preliminary sniffing around as dogs are wont to do, began trying to tug her purse (and her along with it) out the door.

No one was more surprised than Miss Om. Presumably, her brain waves—alpha ones, to be sure—had slowed parallel with her breathing patterns. So intent were the meditators that hardly anyone even realized Bam's efforts at petty theft. Bam began to growl and tug on the purse strap. Instead of experiencing the "other shore" of nirvana, she now experienced a dog who wanted a detour in which to frolic. Instead of the peace that passeth all understanding, she experienced Bam's natural efforts at a play of his own. At first she tried to be congenial, awakened after a peaceful sleep, and was able to push Bam away. But Bam was as relentless as wind-whipped whitecaps pounding for shore.

Sandy nudged Orestes who saw what was going on. He grinned. He had second thoughts about tapping Mark since Mark was in deep meditation, a dream state.

Again Bam made another assault. He tucked in his tongue as he pulled the purse strap away. Again, she was able to get it away from him. Clearly, Miss Om was becoming exasperated, especially as Bam made another attempt. Fortunately, an herbal essence therapist collared Bam and let him out the door. For a twinkling second there was peace on the eastern front.

Miss Om was grateful; she thanked the therapist who in her essence returned to her mandala-shaped frisbee which marked her spot on a nearby mat.

But Bam was not to be denied. Between Oms Bam's panting and sniffing could still be heard outside the door. He wanted that purse in the worst way. Formidable was Bam's determination; a torrent of doggone attraction spurred him on. Continual sniffing was a distraction that kept both Sandy and Orestes from a deep meditative state. Bam's sniffing also kept both Sandy and Orestes aware of what was about to occur. Just as Miss Om was regaining her composure and resuming her deep breathing, someone opened the door and came in. Another latecomer sat down. It was all the incentive—did Bam ever need an incentive?— and space Bam needed. Seeing his opportunity, he slid through the door. Adjusting his eyes to the gathering's subdued light, he soon found the object of his playful tugs.

Again he sunk his teeth into Miss Om's purse. This time she was able to dislodge them from the purse strap and pushed him away brusquely. Again and again he came back. By this time, Miss Om was so disgusted she thought of leaving. She tried swearing at Bam but he was not deterred. So determined was he that he actually managed to knock her out of the full-lotus position. This began to attract the notice of several others who were increasingly caught up in the commotion. At length her swearing grew louder, even to the point of referring to Bam as a "son of a bitch." Now she was taking swings at Bam.

First a right cross to the upper torso stunned him. Then a sweeping motion with her arm rolled him over on his side. In a flash, he had the purse again. More punches. Now karate chops. More swearing. Miss Om was exasperation itself. Forget nirvana! Forget peace! Forget cosmic unity! Not today! Bam was on the loose!

All the while Mark was in deep meditation, undeterred by all the distractions. Neither Orestes nor Sandy bothered to disturb him, even if they could. He was in another world; one might say he was a thousand lives away.

After several more forays, and after Miss Om was thoroughly disgusted because her alpha waves had been distracted by Bam's resurgent efforts at petty theft, this time a primal scream therapist and a tarot card-sex therapist came to her rescue. Bam was thrown out the door. The primal scream therapist suggested she make a primal scream to relieve her stress; Miss Om told her she was in no mood to assume a fetal position to do so.

Sandy and Orestes grinned at all this. The chorus of Ommmmmm Ommmmmmm Ommmmmmm Ommmmmmm continued as though nothing had happened. Mysore and company were tranquil and thoroughly concentrated on the relentless repetition of Ommmmmmm Ommmmmmmmmm.

Miss Om gathered her sweater and now partially-torn purse strap and noticed that in all of his pawings Bam had put a hole in her bag of granola. This only added to her misery. Saving what granola she could, she left this platonic cavern. Fortunately, she left by an exit on the opposite side of the gym. It was worth the effort. There is no telling what would have happened had she gone out the same door where Bam was still sniffing around. Her purse, with all its scents, would have been chewed to shreds. As it was, he remained there sniffing for quite awhile.

They never saw Miss Om again, and, as they left campus, wondered if she had ever found any kind of peace. As for Bam, he was not sniffing too long at the gym door; nor was this pooch waiting with anticipation for some unwitting latecomer. He continued his search for play and frolic, since every distraction has its attractions, in another light.

The Incident at Zeno's Hideaway

Our private lives, later or sooner, may become an open book. Take this diary, for instance:

1981
page 14

Gabe (he does not like to be called Gabriel) told me he wants out of his marriage. He's only staying in it for the sake of his children. He says he has an obligation to stay with his wife. But we *will* be married soon. You'll see. I have that kind of effect on him. I can be exceptionally persuasive. Besides, staying in a marriage for the sake of his children is not a good reason. It just makes Gabe miserable. I wonder if Penelope feels the same way. I doubt it. Gabe is quite a mover and shaker; the glitter, the powerful all get to me. I have never been around someone like that before.

page 29

Gabe is restless; he's tired of making love on the sly. I've enjoyed being with him. He opens me like a flower. Penelope must be a bore or a witch. She's so demanding on him. Gabe is so giving; my new diamond stick pin is so compelling. I just know we'll be getting married. Last week he promised: "We will get engaged soon." But he balks at the talk of marriage. I just know we'll be getting married.

1984
page 69

Gabe says I look beautiful in my new bikini and pearl necklace he gave me for my twenty-eighth birthday. So far, his wife does not suspect anything. According to Gabe, Penny is so boring he can hardly stand it. He has to move his family because he is being transferred to California by his company. I plan to follow him. I can't conceive of life without him. My friend Lilith says I am crazy for getting involved with an older married man in the first place. "You will end up a broken heart," she tells me over and over. She does admit Gabe is indeed handsome. He becomes more handsome with each of the gifts he brings to our love. What more could a woman want?

1987
page 101

In three years I have seen Gabe only five times. I'm now thirty-two; my biological clock is ticking away. I cherish the diamond earrings he gave me for our sixth anniversary. I've never been so in love and in so much pain at the same time. Love can scar beyond recognition. To hold him even if for only a day...I really want to be married. We would have a wonderful life together. If only Penelope would divorce him or just leave. She stands between me and the one I love. Why would she want to stay around anyway? Gabe told me their marriage was over long ago. She's so demanding. Nags him all the time...about everything. No wonder he wants out.

1989
page 192

Listening to the song "Diamonds and Rust": Love that song. My life seems adrift. I have seen Gabe only five times in the last year. He keeps closer to his family. They even go on vacations together. I'm in California; I don't know many people and the ones at work are only work friends. And they always seem to be going to wine and cheese tastings. You'd think they'd be drunk or at least high most of the time. Some of them are. I don't do much but sit by the phone. Gabe does not return my calls. Yet I sit by the phone, hoping and hoping. So lonely. Can it be that love can turn into its opposite? I don't want to think about it. The diamond necklace he gave me the last time we were together is gorgeous. I just love diamonds. I thought by now we would be married. But that...is more and more a mirage.

My job now requires that I occasionally fly out of state. I leave word with Gabe and hope Penelope does not have access to his private phone. He does not return my calls. Maybe she knows and erases my messages! That witch! She stands between me and the one I love. That other day I was in town and I swear I saw a woman who looks just like my friend Lilith. I should have gone over and at least introduced myself. But then I thought: "What if it *is* her? What would she be doing out here in California? I called her number that night; it has been disconnected. She's never approved of my pursuit of Gabe. She used to say: "He will nail you. You'll never forgive yourself."

1990
page 232

I am thirty-five and counting. Gabe gave me a diamond "engagement" ring. The word "engagement" does not ring too well with me. We've been lovers too long. I still want a family. He always changes the subject. He says: "As I've told you before, Chance, I have an obligation to my family. Please try to understand that." He's so cute and sincere. I love the way his smile tilts in the corner of his mouth. To me, he's a prince of this world.

1993
page 293

I am now thirty-eight. Time is running out. I want a family with Gabe so badly. But he changes the subject whenever I mention commitment and marriage. In the last three years I have been with him four times. Both of his kids are in college. At times my anger is on the breaking point. At times I hate him. Once I became desperate. I called him at home. Penelope answered the phone. I just hung up. I've done that dozens of times over the past two years. One moment my love is sustained; the next I hate him for all the delays. I have let him put my life on hold. I miss talking with

Lilith. The letters to her always return. She has no forwarding address.

1995
page 347

Any hopes of marrying Gabe have vanished. He is always gone. He sure is not at home. I did something I never thought I would do. I refused to accept his diamond bracelet. I told him I would gladly accept it if we talked about our future together. He got angry and slapped me hard. I could not believe he slapped me. His hand left its outline on my face. This is the love of my life and he slapped me. I called in sick at work; I did not want anyone to see the bruise on my face. Though I love him still, I am beginning to see what I did not want to see all along.

1996
page 403

Gabe has not returned my calls in several weeks. Finally I called his home—a desperate move since he has always warned me not to call him at home. Penelope answered. I said: "Is Gabriel there?" A long silence. "You must be Lilith," she said. I swallowed hard. "Lilith?" She continued: "Or is it Lashika this time?" I hung up. Stunned. Lilith? My friend Lilith? I sat there like a statue. Licked my lips; my breathing became inconsolable. That was all. I saw my life of waiting fly up like flames. Who is Lashika? Where did she come from?

page 444

Out of desperation or habit, I called Gabe's home. Maybe Penelope would blurt out something about Lilith. She answered the phone: "Is Gabe there?" I said muffling my voice. A long silence. "Who is this? Lashika?" Undeterred, I repeated: "Is Gabe there?" After a moment of silence, she said: "No, he's not here. He's probably with his personal secretary. He just hasn't been the same since his surgery." Stunned, I said: "Surgery?" "Yes, he had a vasectomy. Seems he needs to prove himself now more than ever. Like he's not himself anymore. Well, whoever you are, you're the fool." Then she hung up. I sat back, dazed.

1999
page 513

I have given up hope of marriage and a family. When I brought up the subject the other day, Gabe belted me. It was like the previous times I called his home. It hurts to discover your love is not who he appears to be. He also denied having a vasectomy. He said that was how Penelope handled his absences. He denied knowing anyone named Lilith. He also denied knowing anyone named Lashika. Yet I found out Lashika is his personal secretary. She must be good at taking dictation. She recently accompanied him on the company jet to Kansas City on business. That much I was able to find out. Lies, lies, and more lies. I believe Lilith and Lashika are his playthings. I don't know how Penelope puts up with it. A saint she must be. Next thing you know he'll run for public office where half-truths are doubly essential.

2000
page 666

I have taken up a new sport—deer hunting. I want to be able to nail a deer at two hundred yards. Gale Mafisto, my coach at the rifle range, always compliments me. He says my accuracy is rare, especially among women. I am waiting for hunting season to open. Then I'll have my license. Penelope still stands between me and the one I love. My letters to Lilith still return with no forwarding address. I still call Gabe mostly out of habit. On weekends I have been able to follow him in my car. Last Saturday he and a woman left a bar and went to a small hotel called *The Sleeping Stallion*. I had never seen her before but she *was* wearing diamonds. I began to swear under my breath. I feel so used, so angry, so bitter.

My therapist is terribly helpful.

"Tell me how all this happened," she said one day.

"I've told the police everything. My lawyer. She did the best she could defending me. Even on appeal."

"Tell *me* then." Because she is so helpful, I decided to tell her.

"I had been hit often enough I could not do my job. There were times I just wanted to go back home. But I had none. My father abandoned the family when I was six. Mom died when I was nine. I lived with assorted relatives after that but was not really close to anyone. Then I lost my job. I could not keep pretending. Makeup only goes so far. My jaw was swollen. Gabe was no longer interested. He had found someone new, although occasionally he still gave me gifts such as a sapphire stick pin. I went and pawned it. I was between jobs. Living in limbo."

"Go on."

"One day I called him again--at home. All hell broke loose. He came by my place, broke down the door, and knocked me silly."

"But why did you continue to call? You knew he didn't want that."

"It was habit. With that many years invested. I had given up everything: marriage, family."

"But the warning signs were there all along. You could have cut your losses and walked away. You think you were dazzled by all the attention, the gifts?"

I nodded. "And I was in love."

"You thought you were in love. Love dies on a one-way dead end street."

We began with my therapist—Mary is her name— listening to my complaints about prison food and the way the guards treat us women. We are treated like swine. She asked about the time I decided to take things into my own hands. It is hard for me to talk about it. It seems that's all I have been doing the last few years.

"As I told you, I began lessons at a rifle range. Accuracy was what I wanted—and got. One afternoon Gabe was abusive on the phone, cussed me out, told me never to call again. Suddenly that was it. Hate rose in me, resentment for all the years of abuse...the broken dreams...I went to get my rifle. I wanted to show him, to get back at him. He thought of me as merely ungrateful for all the times and gifts. I drove out to where he usually went, it was a large park, the one where, set off by itself, a couple of miles away. Zeno's Paradox is...it's better known as Zeno's Hideaway."

"Go on," she said.

"He was standing there waiting...as if waiting for someone. I did not care who. Nor was I gonna wait to find out. I lay flat, got him in my sight, and pulled the trigger. I missed him. He had bent down to get his keys. The bullet landed on the other side of him. He dove under a table as I kept shooting. Then I heard someone cry out. The cry distracted me. Quickly he dashed to his car and drove off. Curious, I checked out the source of the cry. I did not want anyone innocent to be hurt. You know, an innocent bystander. I ran over to where the cry came from. At first there was no sign of anyone."

"Go on," said Mary.

"There she was: Lilith. One of the bullets hit her. And she was dead. I was horrified. There were bruises on her face too. I felt so sad, so betrayed. I ran, got in the car, and in a few minutes caught up with him. He was also responsible for my friend's death."

"But it was one of your bullets that killed *her*...right?" she interjected. I nodded sadly.

"He drove to Zeno's Hideaway. He must have known I could catch up with him on the open road. But Zeno's was the most likely place for him to hide. You know about Zeno's?"

"No, refresh my memory. Is that the place where motion does not exist or at least slows down?"

"Yes. It's named after the philosopher Zeno of Elea's Paradox. It's a thick forest that resists and sometimes stops motion. Sometimes it is called Zeno's Paradox."

"Oh, yes. Zeno's Paradox: for anything to go from point A to point B, A would first have to go one half the distance and then one half of that distance and so on. Pretty soon the space gets smaller and smaller so that you can't go from point A to point B. In any case, motion slows down in that thick grove; it is as if the builders *wanted* to make Zeno's Paradox *come true*."

I am amazed how informed Mary is—even in philosophy which can be therapeutic.

"He drove into the driveway leading to Zeno's Hideaway, got out, and once inside the grove disappeared. Parking the car, I followed him. I watched for any slight movement which would tell me where he was. Minutes took forever. Finally there was a detectable movement. Carefully I took aim and fired. The bullet traveled to the edge and, once inside, slowed then stopped in midair. I could see it spinning, suspended and spinning. Then it fell harmlessly to the ground. It took my breath away. I suddenly felt helpless. You don't have to go in far. In fact, it's best if you don't because you get caught up in a more powerful suspended motion."

"Isn't the Paradox shaped like a heart?"

"Yes, you stop at the center of the heart. That is also where time stops. You move faster around the edges. He must have known that because he was only a few feet, if that far, inside."

"He had called someone on his phone. And he waited. I did not know whether he had called the cops or what. It was so frustrating. I didn't want to go into Zeno's just because he might discover me and escape. So I reloaded and waited. Sooner or later, he would have to come out. Shadows of twilight were already deepening. I bet he would try to crawl out and make a run for it. So I waited and waited."

"Go on," said Mary.

"It wasn't long before a car pulled in the long driveway to Zeno's. Hiding behind some shrubs, I could see the car parked next to Gabe's. Guess who steps out but Lashika, another one of his playthings! I did not know what was going to happen so I made sure my rifle was loaded and aimed at Gabe's car. He would have to make a run for it. Curiously, Lashika stood by the car, waiting. She did not even start for the Hideaway. She just stood there, looking around. Then she walked around Gabe's car, stopped for a moment, and gazed all around. She was dressed fit to kill. Something was about to explode. Tension thickened the air. Dusk was beginning to roll in. Next thing I knew there was a rustle near the edge of Zeno's near the bottom of the heart. Suddenly Gabe shot out, running as fast as the wind. But my accuracy was perfect. I had shot a dear at two hundred yards. Shot that dead deer dead."

"Then what happened?"

"He fell just in front of Lashika. Then I heard a second shot. She pulled Gabe to one side, out of my sight. Then, of all things, she started shooting at me! I crawled to the edge of Zeno's just inside the grove."

"A paradox is a blessed refuge sometimes, isn't it?" observed Mary.

"You're telling me. Suddenly I felt I could survive, that her bullets could not reach me. It was weird. Everything slowed down. A strange feeling splashed over me like I was a stranger in a stranger paradox. She fired again. Above me I could hear a bullet; I looked up and it was suspended, spinning and spinning. Then it dropped harmlessly to the ground a few feet away. She knew where I was. It was tempting to venture further into this paradox. I thought she might find me. I listened hard but heard nothing. Then, to my complete surprise, I heard sirens in the distance. Gabe *had* called the cops. I did not know if he had called Lashika. Maybe she had come to hunt him down herself. Holding my breath, I waited to see if she was going to take refuge in Zeno's or try to escape. Paradox *can* be a trap, you know. Sure enough, Lashika got in her car and sped off. The sirens were coming closer. I did not want to stay here at all. Crawling to the edge, I did not see anyone in the driveway. As I was desperately trying to dislodge myself from Zeno's, the cops were already in the driveway. It was too late! I crawled back in. Maybe they would not find me. Several squad cars pulled in. I watched as they discovered Gabe's body and called for paramedics and police backup. I was trapped. It was just a matter of when I would have to move. Yet here motion was slowed down to almost nothing. Police dogs, the German Shepherds, sniffed me out. Cops soon surrounded Zeno's. There was no way out. Sometimes I feel like a coward. Surrendering to them. And then seeing those headlines the next day: *Executive Gabriel Love Killed In Ambush Near Zeno's Hideaway; former mistress captured*...But...here I am."

Mary was silent for awhile.

"You still have time to do."

"I've wasted my life."

"You haven't wasted your life. If you have not learned from this, maybe you have...We'll get together again soon. In the meantime, here's a thought you can take with you."

Again she gave me her calling card on which was printed:

Mary Amida, Ph.D., D.D.
Reality Therapy and East-West Counseling

On the other side was a typed-in quote:

As with the depths of a diamond,
the interior is twice as important as the surface.
There are people who are all facade...
-*Baltasar Gracian*

Over the years I have learned to accept as well as to give other kinds of gifts. They are what matter. Who knows, despite the guilt and the anger, maybe I can find my way out of almost any paradox.

Category Mistake

Doors to the emergency room swung open. Professor Cooper Kent was wheeled in as nurse Dana announced the situation to the staff on duty. "Fifty-two year old male. Collapsed at work. Contusions to the left arm and injury to the head."

Cooper Kent was soon hooked up to tubes and being attended to. He seemed quite fatigued and somewhat disoriented. His wife, Eva, had arrived soon after he was in the hospital. For several moments, she held his hand and then sat down by his bed.

As Dr. Thorne came in, she looked to him for some sense of what had happened. Dr. Thorne was an efficient, no-nonsense, cost-effective physician who seemed to downplay what had happened to Professor Kent.

"We're just running some routine tests now, Mrs. Kent. Seems he became dizzy and just lost his balance. That's when he collapsed. We're not sure whether he simply had some kind of —" he said as his voice dropped off. Then he resumed: "Our tests will tell the tale."

"I'm just glad his students notified the paramedics. Then I got a call from the college."

"The sooner we can do something, the better," observed Dr. Thorne. "I agree," said Dr. Susan Elazar, who had just come into the room.

Dr. Thorne, with faint disgust on his face, left the room. Nurse Dana came in. He gave Kent some pills to take to ease the pain and continued to check the bandage on the professor's head.

"Mrs. Kent, would you like anything to eat? Or drink?" offered Dana.

"Not right now. Maybe later," said Eva, somewhat distracted.

"If you do, we have a cafeteria one floor up. The elevator is right down the hall."

Dr. Elazar continued to check Professor Kent's medical history and to go over it with Eva. Not only did Kent have a history of high blood pressure but was overweight and in dire need of adequate exercise. It turned out Kent had, in various stages, a case of hardening of the arteries and this incident had manifested the symptoms. After Dr. Elazar left the room, Eva went to the cafeteria and bought a salad, blue berry muffins, red grapes, and slices of orange for Cooper and herself.

It was not long before Kent's colleague, Jerome Kegger, came for a visit. It was somewhat odd that they would be collegial at all since Kegger and Kent were from opposite positions philosophically. Kegger leaned more in the direction of European continental philosophy and Kent was an entrenched partisan of the tradition of philosophical analysis. At times they traded barbs and even put downs. But they still were friends because they each possessed a scintilla of skepticism that prevented them from being dogmatic about their philosophical persuasions. He goes down the hall to the nurse's station and sees Eva talking to nurse Dana. She interrupts her conversation.

"Hi, Jerome. Glad you could come by," said Eva, who looked drained with fatigue.

"How is he?" asked Jerome.

"They're running some tests. Just hurt himself when he fell and hit his head."

"That's what I heard. Anything I can do?"

"Not really. He'll be glad to see you. Dr. Elazar thinks hardening of the arteries may be the culprit."

They go further down the hall to Kent's room.

"Hello, Coop. Thought I'd come by to say hello and cheer you up."

Cooper Kent smiled to see his longtime pesky colleague.

"I'm waiting. So far, I'm not cheered up, Kegger."

Jerome smiled. Eva sat in a corner of the room. She scanned the room as the two philosophers talked and then stared outside. It was raining in the fading light of the late afternoon sun.

Soon Drs. Thorne and Elazar came in to go over notes and make some changes. They entered in the middle of a conversation between Kent and Kegger on the soul and its expression in the human being. The doctors could not help but overhear their conversation.

"Well, you know what my theory is...if there's a soul, let's operate," declared Dr. Thorne.

"We might need to," declared Jerome.

"Let's assume for the sake of healing, there is one," Dr. Elazar shot back. Dr. Thorne's face showed contempt for his colleague. He had disapproved of a new requirement in medical schools and hospitals for developing a bedside manner and empathy for patients and their families. As far as he was concerned, you just did your job and let those concerns be addressed within the family. But sometimes families did not care for the patient because of ignorance or an uncaring attitude. Dr. Elazar approved of the new requirement, since she had always shown empathy in her dealings with patients and their families. She and Dr. Thorne had clashed before on other issues.

"Why don't you take this case, Dr. Elazar. Be sure to show your empathy," he said with slight sarcasm. And with that, he left the room. Susan was glad to see him leave.

"Nothing like collegiality," observed Jerome.

"Nothing like it. We obviously have our differences," Susan Elazar mused. She began to go over the latest test results. It was indeed a hardening of the arteries and a mild depression.

"I think it is a hardening of the categories," asserted Jerome.

"A hardening of the categories?" asked Susan.

"Yes, the philosopher's disease. From what I have observed and thought there are several categories: lines, quantity, streams, quality, states, relation, waves, and modality."

"I wouldn't know anything about that," mused Susan. "That's a totally different category. We don't treat a hardening of the categories. A hardening of the arteries, for sure."

"Why do you think he had a hardening of, as you say, categories? I'm curious."

"Well, you just become entrenched in what you do. Your mind becomes static.

You specialize and reap the rewards of specialization but become convinced that there is little outside of that that is worthy of your attention."

"But you have to specialize, don't you?"

"Yes, but the downside is that it closes you off. And ever since we, that is, our faculty, have begun teaching world philosophy, rather than just western philosophy, he's been frustrated and upset about it. That means he has had to teach someone other than David Hume whom he thinks is the greatest philosopher in the history of the British Isles."

"But isn't it good to know other philosophies?" queried Susan.

"Of course. But now he has to learn and teach Shankara of India, Nishida Kitaro of Japan, Mao Tse Tung and Wang Yang Ming of China, the deified heart of Mexico's Aztecs, Muhammad Iqbal of India, negritude of colonized Africa and so forth. And Coop does not like it one bit."

"Let's not get on that again," said Kent with a slight wave of his arm. He had been over this issue with Jerome Kegger many times.

"You know I have seniority. I shouldn't have to teach such stuff as Ken Wilber's Integral Theory or the thought of Aurobindo. Who can compare with the western rational/analytic philosophical tradition, including Hume? No one."

"But even Hume," ventured Jerome, "borrowed from Buddhism's doctrine of no- eternal soul or self. And causality was attacked by Persia's Al-Ghazali long before Hume was playing backgammon or whist."

"You don't have to be depressed about such things," suggested Eva. "Yes, just think of it as a new learning experience of our life here in the cosmos," added Jerome.

Cooper just said Hrrmmph under his breath.

Eva knew her husband had been depressed lately but did not have a clue as to why he would be. After all, he had finished his book on proving the existence of other minds. An article on Hume's attack on the design argument for the existence of God had been published in the prestigious *Skeptical Review* and had received mixed reviews since it has a wide readership among skeptics who were skeptical about Hume's skepticism. He had been invited later that spring to be the keynote speaker at the smoker for the Philosophical Narration and Knowledge Society. Things were going very well for Cooper Kent. And yet he was sad and now diagnosed as mildly depressed. The new course in world philosophy seemed to be a factor. But an inquisitive mind usually does not remain static or even departmental. It would be like a physics student denying the existence of quarks or anti-matter.

She and Jerome left the room to get some food from the cafeteria. On the way, Jerome put forth another explanation. He saw Cooper as a die-hard partisan for whom narrowness garnered the rewards of philosophy. He had specialized as a young man and had given up on the youthful idea that philosophy had much more to offer than clarifying concepts and discussing issues that were raised by new scientific discoveries. Cooper Kent had gone into philosophy with the idea that its domain was inventive, encompassing, and able to assert an influence far beyond the classroom. Gradually, over the years, he had forgotten that idea as he received one award after another by circumscribing his vision and marginalizing the relevance of philosophy. His students noticed this too. When he first started teaching, he was in touch with his students and had not become as yet set in his ways or, as they say, a hardening of the categories. But now, there was nothing to deal with outside his specialty except an occasional pesky Jerome Kegger who kept reminding him from time to time that philosophy must do more than sit on the sidelines and play a reactive marginal role with regard to the other fields of knowledge and experience. Cooper Kent found this at best annoying, at worst a betrayal of the tidbit approach to selected problems that philosophy could modestly comment on or analyze in terms of the best arguments. He knew philosophy had narrowed itself so that the types of issues and questions were limited by its own self-limiting concerns and he did not want to make a category mistake by assuming that another department of knowledge would take offense or pronounce him incompetent if he took such fields into account when he did do philosophy. At some level, this very success thus far had both exhilarated him and depressed him. He knew he had lost something along the way. A vague feeling that even in his research and teaching highlights something was missing, bothered him in those moments of solitude when one gains a sense of perspective that does not intrude itself in the quavering distractions that so often are the diet of everyday life.

Susan Elazar recommended that Cooper remain in the hospital for the night. Eva was shocked at how much it would cost to stay in the hospital; she wanted to have Cooper released so she could care for him at home. Susan made sure Cooper went home with all the appropriate meds the next day. It was not long before a gradual change began to take place in Cooper Kent's classes. He seemed more in touch with his students. His evaluations went up and he began to learn to learn again, to remain open to world philosophy and to discover aspects of his consciousness that had been numb for several years. He even began to be less grudging against his old friend, Jerome Kegger. No longer did he dismiss Kegger's philosophical leanings as "full of bullology" or even Kegger's interest in robots, dream therapy, and firewalking. In time, Cooper even began to think of his fall as prophetic to once again see the world in a wise to the wise perspective.

The Hook

"Don't drink all that stuff. It's an import," warned James as he took his fishing gear and headed over the gentle hill to the leeward side of Lake Berryessa. "I'll probably come get some more." The label on the bottle read Old Adam's Ale.

"You don't think I'd drink all *that*, do you?" I replied. He grinned but made no reply as he disappeared. Our boat was tied to a low-hanging limb.

As morning broke, lupines carpeted the northern flank of hills. Clouds wispy here and there mapped the sky. Clusters of mustard waved bright yellow in the breezes of spring. Fishing was slow; I wondered how James was faring as I took another swallow. After awhile, I began to feel light-headed. If you don't get a bite, take another swallow of that stuff, I thought. And so I did. Fishing was deep since spring warmth had sent the trout and bass deeper, sometimes into the shadows. Morning drowsily eased into afternoon.

I baited my hook again and cast in. Looking up, I saw a man in a kayak wearing a funny hat on his head. It turned out to be an admiral's hat with a long red plume flowing from it. The kayak turned in my direction. As it drew near our boat, the man barked:

"Have you seen my fleet?"

"Your what?" I said.

"My fleet," he said. He noticed I was staring at his hat and he offered: "Oh, this," he pointed to his hat, "I am an admiral."

"An admiral?"

"Yes. And I have lost my fleet," he added as though this was of utmost importance.

"You've lost your fleet?"

"Yes. Have you seen it? Schooners, two-masted clipper ships."

"No. I haven't seen any fleet around here. This is only a lake, a mirage. No fleet could fit here."

He was now close enough so I could see his thick sideburns, muttonchops, and dark mustache; they were not quite as prominent as his plume that fluttered in the breeze. After a long, almost meditative pause, he said "'Tis no mirage, sir. I must be off to find my fleet." I nodded in agreement. It sounded like a splendid idea.

"Yes, you must be off...Good luck," I said. Off came his admiral's hat. In a courtly gesture, he bowed until his lips almost touched the kayak. Soon he rounded a point of rock just off shore and disappeared. I baited my hook again and cast in. Not long afterwards, I noticed another boat round the bend in the cove. In it a gorilla leisurely rowed, each oar glistening in the sun. He saw my boat and began rowing toward mine.

I looked at what I'd been drinking with its wordless brown paper cover then returned my eyes toward this boat in which sat someone dressed as one of the higher primates.

Our eyes met. He tried to make gestures, such as scratching, to make it seem he was really an ape. Why would anyone dress up as one of the higher primates on a warm spring day and row around this particular portion of the lake? I made up my mind not to say anything.

With barely a sound, his boat nudged mine. Not once did this person's eyes veer from mine. We were in a staring contest. I swallowed hard; I did not know what was going to happen or what would be said. Scratching himself, he continued to stare at me then finally extended his hand and began to pat me down as though looking for a concealed weapon. Was this a stop and frisk situation? There was no probable cause! Why, I was both a fisherman and a taxpayer! This disgusting beast was apparently going to carry this charade as far as he could. That I was becoming upset was obvious. Yet mingled with my disgust was a faint curiosity.

"Get your paws off me," I demanded.

His eyes darted to mine and riveted on them as it stopped pawing me. For the first time, I noticed letters on the mud-caked bow of his boat LETHE as though his boat had been turned over in the waters of oblivion. My eyes returned grimly and steadily to his.

"What on earth do you want?" I demanded again. No reply.

By now his hairy paws were back in his boat yet his eyes remained riveted to mine.

"What do you want? Are you deaf?" The gorilla shook its head. Finally a response! For a moment, I thought I was going to scream.

His voice was slow and deliberate, a baritone. "I'm searching this body for..." he said gesturing toward the lake. Whatever apprehension that had begun to show itself in me began equally as fast to disappear.

"For what?" I asked. "What are you looking for?" I repeated. Seconds oozed like molasses in snow.

"The primitive," he replied finally. Enough was truly enough, I thought.

"Oh, the primitive," said I. "That's further down the lake around that point of rock. You'll see a fisherman. His name is James."

"That's where you need to look," I continued. "No primitive here."

No humor rose in those eyes. Only wonderment. His head leaned over as though he were listening for something far away, as of surf breaking on a distant shore. Distance outlined his eyes, an almost misty-eyed rendezvous.

"Truly, the primitive is not here," I repeated. The gorilla nodded as though sad.

He too must have known beneath his hairy coat, in his humorless eyes, the primitive had to be somewhere further away.

"Why can't you simply be a man?" I asked with a sudden, almost unintended curiosity.

"I am not a man. I no longer wish to be. I am a gorilla searching for my home."

His denial struck me as peculiar, especially since he obviously *was* a man inside a gorilla suit.

He thanked me, slipped his oars into the lake, and slowly rowed away. As his boat pulled away, I could make out what seemed to be the boat's full and complete name "Haletheia" printed on the aged stern. Later it was disclosed to my amazement that "Haletheia" was the Greek word for "truth." A vague feeling flowed over me that I would see him again, perhaps on another shore.

His boat soon rowed out of sight; I breathed easier; and now, finally, looked forward to doing some serious fishing on a lazy afternoon. I mused how two people had interrupted this fishing trip. My thoughts turned to James. I wondered if that ape had actually gone to visit him.

Smiling, I thought how it would be for James to have an ape row up to him while he was fishing. Oh, well, I would talk to him later. This lunatic's brew tasted good going down. My toes wiggled in the sunshine; I wanted to get a bass or trout on the line. So far no fish. After baiting again my hook, I cast in.

It was not long before I noticed, to my surprise, another boat round the bend in the cove. I did not believe what I was seeing. Maybe James was playing tricks on me. He had done so before; pranks were his game, especially when his girlfriend Zelda was with him. I rubbed my eyes not once but three times. Each time they saw the same things. There must be some kind of masquerade party going on, I mused. In the distance I could make out what appeared to be a large bird rowing toward me. In fact, it resembled a larger-than-life chicken. My first impulse was to leave. Now. Get out now before another strange bird appeared. But the concoction I had been drinking had slowed me down so that my arms could not obey the impulses from my brain. As its boat neared mine, it became rather apparent that this was no ordinary bird. It was none other than someone dressed as the Crazy Chicken, a bird peculiarly suited to large crowds at professional ball games. This fowl was famed for giving foul hugs and even kisses to total strangers. Yet here there was not a crowd unless you counted the trout, bass, bluegill, and catfish. At ball games, this bird was wont to run madly like some reveling dionysian among the beer drinkers and hot dog lovers and embrace them with its rubbery beak. Visions of such scenes oppressed me as this fowl-burdened boat edged its way toward mine. It had been an eventful day and the prospect of being given a life-smothering bear hug by a man-sized barnyard resident did not excite me in the least. Slowly, ever so slowly, its boat inched closer.

Thoughts of a lazy afternoon of serious fishing began to flee one fish at a time. At this point I could have caught a blue marlin off Cabo San Lucas and it would hardly have phased me. Somehow, in the midst of this moment, I wanted to be almost anywhere but here. With Ernest Hemingway at the running of the bulls in Pamplona; on the veranda with

William Faulkner at Rowan Oak; with Kitagawa Utamaro pouring over the purity and beauty of Japanese maidens; with Fyodor Dostoevsky in the middle of Father Alyosha's prayer; with Meister Eckhart preaching to a gathering of nuns at Strasbourg. Anywhere but here.

Just then the chicken stood up and opened its arms as if to hug a long, lost cousin. Bracing myself, I gave it as cold a stare as I could. Some fishing trip, I thought.

"You must be a fan," clucked the chicken, anticipating a country club celebration.

"Oh, no, I'm not. Not me. I don't follow a team," I said. The chicken appeared perplexed like a lawyer who has misplaced her briefs.

"Everyone's a fan of someone," averred the chicken.

"Not everyone," I replied emphatically.

"Even if you're not, you must know me."

"No," I teased. "I don't know who you are at all. Is this a masquerade?"

For a moment the chicken seemed almost downcast.

"I'm the Crazy Chicken. My lawyer just got me a patent on this suit. I rally the team. Hug the bottle-throwing fans!"

"Pleased to meet you," I said, extending my hand. I shook its right wing which was somewhat limp as though lacking in right wing enthusiasm.

"Tell me, are you a he or a she?"

"A she, but many think I'm a he. Some even wish I were only a he," she said, her comb tilted to one side.

"Well, as long as you know who you are, then you've no problems, right?" Expecting the chicken to concur, I breathed easier. However, the chicken demurred.

"You can have problems even if you don't. But fortunately I do know who I am. I am a chicken...and proud of it," she said, as her comb tilted now to the other side.

I thought no one on this lake seems to know who they are. I was delighted to be one of the few on the lake who could say I knew who I was. Or was I?

The chicken luckily did not hear my thoughts. I grew more curious.

"Why do you think you're a chicken," I said after a pause.

"Because I'm loved as a chicken. The crowds...they love me."

"Who knows? Maybe you can be loved as a human being, too," I said with an assurance that came from where I did not know.

"You really think so?" she asked as though she were a doll whose arms had been twisted by great expectations once too often.

"Why don't you take off that silly mask?" I ventured. Her red comb swung now over to the other side of her head.

"But you may not like me the way I'm used to...It's just easier to keep it on. Then no one knows who's hugging them as they wolf down their hot dogs and beer. You know how it is with high culture. It's just the play, you know," she said, her plastic eyes big with excitement, as big as one can become within the limits of plastic.

"Oh, c'mon," I prodded, drinking some more of Old Adam's Ale. My aim was to keep this chicken so distracted she would not try something so foolish as to climb in my boat and give *me* a hug or a kiss as though *I* were a fan.

The chicken shook her head. "It takes the fun out of it," she averred.

"I'd really like to know the 'real' you," I said. "I bet you're a nice chicken, I mean person."

"Really, it's much easier this way," declared the chicken. With that she moved closer. Before I could say "unmask that chicken" she had given me a big hug and kiss. That's how close our boats were.

"I didn't really want a hug. Or a kiss for that matter. I'm not even a fan."

"Oh, I know," she bubbled. "But you looked like you needed them. Anyway, time to go. The crowds are waiting, you know. Fame calls."

My relief at watching her boat pull away was nothing short of gargantuan; it had been a somewhat bizarre afternoon. And I had no fish, not even a bite. What would James think? Only the lupines that blanketed the meadows redeemed the day for me. Her boat soon disappeared around that same point of rock. Maybe I should go and find James before another sideshow floats up here, I thought. At first I had difficulty getting out of the boat for my muscles had not moved much in the last few hours. Up the hill I climbed at a slow pace then turned around and gazed back at the boat. Reaching the crest of the hill, I paused again and felt the slight breeze. So far, there was no sign of James at least where I thought he would be fishing. Through a thick portion of tall grass, there was another clearing; moving cautiously and curiously, I came to another path that wound down on the other side of the hill until it came to a clearing. Finally James! His line was in the lake but next to him was the admiral's hat, dancing plume and all. A couple of steps to my right, behind a low-slung branch clustered with leaves, I spied a kayak. The same kayak, the same admiral's hat.

Puzzled, and with a deepening frown, I paused to gather what thoughts I could. What has been going on here? I did not want to think it really was a set of pranks. From behind some tall grass emerged a woman. I stared intently. So familiar it was his girlfriend, Zelda, who sat down next to him. Where did she come from? Maybe that road, that service road, that curved down the hill, the one that was used for fire trucks, was how she came into the scene. Or maybe by boat. But whose boat?

Beneath my puzzled thoughts, I had this sudden gut feeling that between those two, my fishing trip had been one long prank. After all, it was only a month ago that James came to my birthday party dressed as Giggles the Clown, claiming my parents had hired him, which was not true. Disgusted and embarrassed, I squatted low and moved slowly for a better view; I did not see anything but the kayak and the admiral's hat. But wait. A gust of breeze came up and curled into sight was a rowboat but there was no lettering on the stern which spelled the Greek word for "truth." Perhaps the "truth" had been erased.

At this point I decided to leave, to just leave all the gear and bottles in the boat, and make my way back to the resort where we had rented the boat. Making sure no one saw me, I ventured back, past the boat that swayed slightly in the breeze, and trudged up the hill behind the cove that led down into a shallow valley already criss-crossed by the setting sunlight. In the distance, I could see the cafe and resort with the boats tied to three docks that protruded out into the lake and a few people mingling there and here as a small cabin cruiser leaving its wake made its way past the harbor buoy toward the deeper part of the lake.

Soon I'll be sitting at that café, coffee in hand, a clearing in my head, waiting with satisfaction on my face. To see the looks on their faces when James and Zelda go to an empty boat only to find me gone. Now that would be worth framing, a hook worth waiting for.

A Summer in the Lives of Two Rebels

It was a momentous summer as far as summers go at age fourteen. It was the summer before freshman football at Ridgeview High. Jon lived less than a mile away from Gazali. Jon's house was easier of access since his parents both worked, his barbells did not have to be undone after each workout, nor did the freezer have to be locked, especially if you liked strawberry ice cream the way Jon and Gazali did that summer. Nevertheless they would usually begin the day with a friendly phone call about who should bike to whose house.

"Jon," Gazali would ask.

"Hi, Jon."

"You wanna workout?"

"Yeah," was the California answer.

"You sound enthused."

"It's almost ninety degrees already."

"The ride will do you good," suggested Gazali, already knowing Jon's reply.

"That's what you think," replied Jon, unenthused.

"C'mon. Why don't you ride up here?" Gazali repeated.

There was a pause. Gazali knew Jon was considering his invitation.

"I don't feel like pedaling all the way up there. It's too hot. It is in the nineties already," Jon observed finally as he watched television from the phone room.

"C'mon. You said you wanted to get in shape. Now you don't want to even peddle up here. 'It's too hot,'" Gazali mimicked his friend's excuses for the past week. "It's in the nineties. I could die of heatstroke," protested Jon whose attention was divided between the phone and TV.

"What a crock," came the nauseated voice on the other end, "I can't believe...what're you gonna do when it's hot on the field? Ask for a timeout? I bet you can't even peddle up here in less than five minutes," challenged Gazali, "that's how out of shape you are." Jon could not resist this challenge to his athletic prowess.

"I bet I can," enthused Jon, now determined.

"Okay," Gazali said deliberately, "I know...I'll time you."

"You're on. Be right there." As he hung up, a broad smile lit Gazali's face. Like a springing panther, Jon hung up, put on his tennis shoes, hopped on his bike, and zoomed down the sidewalk. As he rode, waves of heat quivered like coiling cobras from the Foster Road asphalt. As his bike cruised onto the gravel of 1251 Foster Road, he eyed his watch. At the top of the driveway stood his friend, at six-three, one hundred and seventy five pounds.

"Took you five minues and thirty-two seconds."

"Bull," retorted Jon, huffing. "By my watch it was four minutes and forty-two seconds," he averred.

"You're not even in shape. And after all we've done this summer." Jon sputtered, still breathing heavily.

"You're not going to be a Y.A. Tittle or a Johnny Unitas this year if you don't get in shape," warned Gazali who enjoyed ribbing Jon.

"Well, you're not exactly Frankie Albert of Stanford or Rockne of Notre Dame either," countered Jon who happened to a have finished a biography of Rockne and was especially impressed with how Rockne and end Gus Dorais had spent the summer of 1913 perfecting the forward pass, a technique that would enable Notre Dame to beat Army 35-13 that season.

"You can't even bench press three hundred," continued Gazali, trying to goad him.

"I bet I will before the season starts," Jon replied as he parked his bike in the shaded area of the breezeway. Going to Gazali's house was sporting because of the fish pond that lay behind the breezeway. Two geese stroked lazily around the pond. They nibbled at bamboo leaves from the bamboo that leaned over the southern edge of the pond. Gazali owned a pair of Toulouse geese and one Embden, a half-breed that formed a ménage a trois. Cautious was Jon's approach when the gander named Senator Stone was present since the gander had once nabbed him by the pant leg and did not turn him loose until Gazali distracted it by holding his even more tantalizing foot out and the gander switched attack: it left the flimsy pant leg for the firmer target of Gazali's athletic foot.

Fortunately for Jon, the gander was stroking around the pond, pausing now and then to honk at the other geese. The Embden, named Daisy, was standing on one foot with her head tucked beneath her feathers and between her folded brown and white wings.

"Stone won't bother you," advised Gazali, referring to the gander as he eyed Jon's concern. "He's in the water." Jon breathed a faint sigh.

Into Gazali's house they went. A fan hummed, TV images danced, and Gazali's mother cut out a recipe from her favorite magazine.

"Hi Dawn," said Jon. Gazali's mother was always it seemed, trying out new and different recipes. She was now cutting out a variation of a recipe for fettucini alfredo.

"Hello, Jon. Nice to see you again. How are you?"

"Fine, Dawn," was the perfunctory answer. Ever curious was Jon about Gazali's mother: she always seemed to be collecting things and never throwing them away. Jon especially liked her homemade pizza. There was always the outside chance, even in summer, of a pan of pizza emerging from the oven. Mouth-watering thoughts diverted him from the conversation. He envisioned one of Dawn's pizzas in his mind: each succulent slice of hot pizza, topped with spicy chunks of Italian sausage, steamed mushrooms tucked between melted blankets of mozzarella, cheddar, and swiss (he swallowed hard at the thought) the long juicy steamed green peppers alluringly basked atop the thick mozzarella and tomato sauce tapestry, the steamed yet firm onions, and chewy yellow crust that made her pizza a pizza lover's dream. It was the stairway to pizza heaven and he would be the first to climb it. In fact, Gazali often wondered whether Jon liked to peddle to his house to see him or his mother. Gazali noticed Jon frequently dropped hints about how scrumptious the last pizza had been, how Gazali's mother was an accomplished cook, and how pizza was one of his favorite all-time foods, especially if an athlete wanted to make the Ridgeview varsity, something Jon had worked for from dawn to dusk throughout the long days of summer.

"You collecting recipes again, Dawn?" he asked, returning to the conversation.

"Yes, it's my hobby. I just love to cook," she replied. She finished cutting out the recipe.

47

"I really like your pizza," declared Jon.

"How well I know," she smiled. "You had six pieces last time. Remember?"

Jon nodded with a grin.

"I'll make it again soon. Maybe tonight. I'll make sure Gazali tells you." Gazali glanced knowingly at Jon.

"You can count on him being here for your pizza," was Gazali's only comment as they left for the bunkhouse which was across a breezeway connected to the main house. Between its knotty pine walls lay window seats, a shelf lined with football, basketball, and baseball stories, two bunk beds, a barbell set, and Gazali's bike with the handle bars turned upside down in racing position.

"I can press one hundred and seventy-five pounds," Gazali said with pride. "My uncle, Seymour, thought this weight program would do the trick. He played for Stanford, you know," he continued as he stooped, set the barbells, and using the power thrust in his knees, straightened and pressed the barbell over his head. He inhaled deeply with a resounding whooshing sound. Up, down, up, down he pressed the barbell.

Then it was Jon's turn. He, too, was able to press the barbell, a fact which impressed Gazali.

"You're getting the strength. You couldn't do that in June," said Gazali, amazed. "You've been practicing..."

"All summer. Your place. Mine. Even at night," came Jon's reply.

"Need power in the wrists," as he watched the barbell go above Jon's head for the third time.

"You've got the breathing down," noted Gazali. "Power's on the exertion."

Jon had been practicing diligently, even at night. It was a fact which impressed Gazali. Not that Gazali had not been working as hard. It was just that Jon's progress was dramatic: in June he had found it hard to press even ninety pounds.

"We'll give the older players something to think about," declared Jon as he envisioned a 39-14 blowout of rival Redwood, wearing a self-entertained smile.

"I plan to start at left end. That's what my dad played at college in Socorro, New Mexico."

"He played baseball, too, didn't he?" asked Jon in a vague yet impressed tone. Jon nodded as his muscles, from biceps to deltoids, tensed in the power phase of the press. He breathed deeply, filling his lungs with a mighty whooshing sound. Although he, too, had worked out almost every day— at least an hour of vigorous exercises and some pumping iron—he continued to be sore.

"Guess what," began Jon who leaned on the top bunk to observe Gazali's straining muscles press over his head. Gazali's eyes veered to Jon's, as if to ask "what?"

"Got a copy of *Look*. The one with Billy Cannon..." he said, referring to the explosive Louisiana State halfback, "and LSU's defensive unit...the Chinese Bandits..."

The barbell now pressed against Gazali's chest when he asked: "You got anymore strawberry ice cream?"

"Didn't you hear me? I got the magazine..."

"I heard you," interjected Jon. "I'd like to see 'ol Billy Cannon..." He feigned a rebel accent. "LSU's got a great team. That's for sure," he said. "But what about the strawberry ice cream?"

"Yeah. Got a whole gallon," answered Jon as he watched Gazali cautiously and properly lower the barbell."

Jon wondered if Gazali really liked venturing to his house because of the spacious workout area or if he simply liked to play with the TV remote control and eat all the ice cream in the house. Jon liked Gazali's mother's pizza; Gazali's liked Jon's mother's supply of strawberry ice cream. Both enjoyed competing. Both enjoyed eating. This made preparation for autumn myths and rituals of the football season both fun and delicious.

After working out with the barbell and arm curls with dumbbells, they both glided on their bikes down the gravel driveway, past the stately eucalyptus tree to Jon's house where they would work out with Jon's set of weights, and leisurely eat smooth spoonfuls of strawberry ice cream.

"Down, Cindy, get down," Jon shouted as they entered the front door. Jon's collie, Cindy, became overly excited whenever anyone, including the milkman, came to the house. So excited would Cindy become she would wet the floor, an event which would cause Jon to attempt broken German swear words: "Ratch me tun mein Hund!" Finally, Cindy settled on the couch with her wet, black nose nestled on her front paws, waiting to spring her shiny-coated legs into action at any moment.

"Let's see what's on TV," suggested Gazali who was fascinated by the new remote control on Jon's TV. As the picture cleared, the announcer asked:

"Would you like to be queen for a day?" The audience roared resounding approval. With a finger flick the channel turned. This was, Gazali thought, an exciting device. Next a news report on San Quentin death row inmate, Carroll Chessman. Then onto a few other game shows until he came to Perry Mason. Intrigued, Gazali became tuned in to the action. He wanted to become a lawyer someday. By contrast, Jon thought the show Hollywoodishly contrived; the series, he thought, had little to do with the usual political paper pushing of a typical law office. Gazali defended it.

"It's just good drama. That's what you'd expect in a good murder case. Think of it as a mystery."

"It's Hollywood. That's for sure," said Jon, skeptical about accuracy. "Lawyers just don't have cases like that very often."

They sat and watched Perry, Della, and Paul for awhile. It was almost noon. It would be time to eat some strawberry ice cream soon. This particular episode of Perry Mason turned on a crucial piece of evidence: a set of footprints that led from a large house to a small nearby cabin were not those of the accused. By showing the prints were not fresh, and identical to those of his client, Perry was trying to prove his client could not have committed the murder of an elderly woman who had been involved in a real estate fraud scheme.

"It's always a key fact. You don't know till the last minute" enthused Gazali who admired Perry's cross-examinations. Jon remained skeptical. Perry won his case; his client, terribly relieved (until he would see Perry's bill) was seen at the end having a drink in Perry's office with Perry, Della and Paul with a couple of volumes of Corpus Juris Secundum on a nearby table.

As usual, Jon was critical. "You can always look good on TV. It's contrived. Real trials are not that cut and dried."

"Yes, but it makes good drama. That's all I'm interested him. Just to be entertained is all I want."

"I think Hollywood distorts everything, that's all. You only see the distortion. It's unreal."

Gazali was not totally tuned in to the conversation and asked vaguely, "What is it you don't like?"

"It's unreal. Not life. As it is. Hollywood is created illusions."

"But that's TV. That's art. It's the only thing we see. It's the drama I like." Gazali was becoming a bit annoyed but realized Jon was probably not in a good mood since he had been having a bad time with his girl, Delilah, lately.

"Say, let's get some ice cream." Gazali's face lit up.

"Yes, let's."

Out to the garage they stepped. Ice vapors curled out of the deep freeze. The ice cream was cold but not too hard. Cindy began barking as the prize was brought to the kitchen drainboard.

"You can't move with the barking," shouted Jon. "She just gets excited." Jon commanded Cindy to cease and desist. Within moments the frisky collie lay on the living room couch, her wet nose propped on her paws. Jon scooped the ice cream into two large dishes. Cindy's ears perked. Her eyes followed her master with beseeching looks.

Cindy caught Jon's eye. He had been trying to avoid her eyes. Avoiding eyes was a way of avoiding interest or obligations. Or feelings of compunction Jon was now experiencing. He grimaced. Cindy's begging moved him. Finally, he rolled a scoop into her dish.

"You're wasting it," Gazali protested.

"Maybe she'll calm down now." Cindy's long pink tongue lapped at the equally pink ice cream. For a moment she was content.

Gazali flicked the TV channel; it was the Brooklyn Dodgers playing the Baltimore Orioles. The Dodgers were taking the field at a change of innings.

"See if Bandstand's on," suggested Jon who sat next to Cindy on the couch. Gazali flicked the remote control. American Bandstand was on: dancers emerged as the camera casually glided among them. Bob Clayton and Justine Carelli turned, spun, bopped, twirled to the delight of fans; the camera panned, passing among dancers as they gracefully passed each, held on to the rhythm and beat of Buddy Holly's *Peggy Sue*.

This is soooooooooooooooooo good," Gazali exclaimed. Heaven was eating ice cream as he savored a strawberry spoonful. He stroked Cindy's shiny coat. Eggs in her diet made her coat shine, a fact of which he was proud.

"You know I sent her a fan letter," continued Gazali.

"Who?"

"Justine."

"Did she write you?"

"Yeah. Sent me a picture."

"Really?"

"One of her and Bob."

Jon laughed. "It figures. She's been with him a couple years." There was a pause as the two of them watched Bandstand.

"How's Delilah?" asked Gazali. Jon sighed a deep one.

"Hard to tell. She changes all the time. One day, yes. Next day, no."

"What do you mean?"

"She doesn't know what she wants."

"Does any girl?" Gazali retorted.

"You know...you're lucky," Jon began again after a pause.

"Why?"

"You don't get serious about 'em."

"When you get involved, it sorta takes over your life. Sports and school are too important."

"And you prefer ice cream. I know. I've heard it before." Jon's involvement with Delilah was not approved by his folks. Just then *Sixteen Candles* by the Crests floated through the room.

"Yeah. But I really like her," Jon said pensively.

"That's up to you. They're too fickle for me," concluded Gazali. He reached over and stroked Cindy, who contentedly basked in the attention of both boys. Gazali longingly watched Justine dance with Bob.

"Her hair is beautiful," Gazali mused as if in a daze or hypnotic trance.

Jon was amused by Gazali's treatment of TV images as if they were real.

"She lives in Philadelphia, Gazali. Do you know how far that is from here? Three thousand miles. She gets all kinds of letters. Yours is just one of the many she gets."

"Don't remind me. But I can love her from afar," Gazali retorted as he stared vacantly at the screen where the blond with long curls and shapely silhouette danced with her equally blond boyfriend.

"It's quite far. That's no lie," mused Jon who was always fascinated with Gazali's idealistic leanings.

Jon disappeared in to the kitchen, refilled their bowls, and returned to the TV room.

"I sometimes think I should break up with Delilah. That would solve a lot of problems. I just can't bring myself..." as his voice dropped off.

"It's not life or death, you know," said Gazali with affected wisdom.

"It's easy for you to say. You like women you'll never meet, like Justine," countered Jon who had had a rough previous night with Delilah. Nights like that sapped his strength.

"That way I don't spend time worrying about how fickle they are." Jon sat there, faintly amused as he too passively gazed at the dancers to the tune of *Oh Donna* by Richie Valens. He too stared at the Italian beauties that seemed abundant in the City of Brotherly Love.

Jon was absorbed in his own thoughts. He remembered the summer dance last week, how he held Delilah close, and how they danced to Earl Grant's song *At the End of a Rainbow*, a song always played at the end of every dance. His heart beat faster and faster until it felt like a huge bullfrog in his throat. He thought he was in love. He wanted her passionately. He felt like a mad poet tiptoeing on star constellations and galaxy seas. He did not believe Gazali would be sympathetic to the ravings of adolescent amours. It was like telling friends of the phantasmagoria of one's dreams. So he kept his best thoughts closest to his heart and limited his comments about Delilah to the mundane.

"You think she loves you?" piped Gazali who was seated under the lamp and perusing in *Look* sensational pictures of Billy Cannon and the Chinese Bandits.

"Sometimes." The Bandstanders now danced to *I Only Have Eyes for You* by the Flamingos.

"She's got you wrapped and you know it," Gazali commented absently. This kind of comment annoyed Jon since it showed Gazali as being insensitive.

"At least I've got a *real* woman, not some screen image like you do. What can you do? You write Justine. And what does she do? She sends you a picture of her *and* her boy friend. At least there's some romance in *my* life," said Jon testily. A long silence. Finally, Jon said: "Let's get off Delilah."

"Cannon has big calves, doesn't he?" asked Gazali who was finally becoming aware of how annoyed Jon had become. Jon nodded as he mindlessly watched Dick Clark begin to have two dancers rate a new release by Little Anthony and the Imperials.

The phone in the study rang. Cindy leaped from the couch and began barking. Gazali finally calmed Cindy down. It was Dawn. Jon's compliments on her homemade pizza had inspired her to make one. She invited Jon to dinner once the pizza had cooled. Jon's mouth watered. He told Gazali and suggested they hold off the ice cream so there might be room for thick slices of pizza casserole.

"I can hardly wait," said Jon enthusiastically. Gazali grinned; he knew how Dawn loved to cook, to gather all the ingredients according to the recipe, then with her unique culinary intuitions vary the amount of basil, add a slightly thicker and deeper red onion-saturated sauce, and add a steamed tangy, green pepper to the already two-inch thick layer of seasoned chunks of meat, mozarella cheese, steamed onions and mushrooms.

"We'd better go lift weights and run some pass patterns because once you get into the pizza you won't be good for nothin'" said Gazali who was quite aware of Jon's appetite. He flicked the TV remote to *Leave It To Beaver*:

"Wally, why do girls do things like show an interest in dancing and stuff," asked the Beaver to his older brother.

"Gee, Beave, I don't know. Maybe they just like dancing the way Eddie likes to come on like he's big stuff with the girls."

"Gosh, Wally, I didn't know Eddie was such big stuff with the girls," said Beaver, puzzled."

"He isn't, Beave. Eddie just thinks he is," concluded Wally as a commercial break left Beaver and Wally in their room to solve another dilemma in the Cleaver household.

"Let's get your football," suggested Gazali who was interested in seeing Jon's room since it was always well-kept. Upstairs he ran ahead of Jon. To the right was Jon's room, across from that of his parents. A desk was on the left, a bulletin board with family and friend photos, and a book shelf for a headboard. Jack London and Ernest Hemingway were two of his favorite authors. On his nightstand was London's novel, *Martin Eden*, with a bookmark halfway through it. Jon would finish it sometime in September so he could turn his entire attention to his school work and his occasional quail hunting trips. By contrast, Gazali was not allowed to have a gun on the premises as his father was a bird fancier who loved his pigeons, Chinese Mandarin ducks, peacocks, geese, mallard ducks, and one turkey. Since he was not that interested in hunting, he did not accompany Jon on his hunting trips.

They rode their bikes to Ridgeview. After a few warm-up and stretch exercises, they practiced their stances and moving at pretended snaps of the ball.

"Put your arm up so you can block...right off the line," commanded Gazali as he watched Jon practice his stance. On the snap, Jon would bull forward, block an imagined defensive end, drift into the secondary in front of imaginary linebackers, catch the ball, and churning his legs, veer across and dart down field.

"Now try down and out," declared Gazali, taking the snap as Jon trotted straight about eight yards and headed toward the sidelines as a perfect spiral landed in his outstretched hands.

"Timing is all. It's everything," commented Jon as he trotted back to the line of scrimmage. He tossed the ball back to Gazali who held it where the imaginary center would snap it.

"Coach Bunch says we're using the single wing this year," said Gazali with authority. "One of the pass patterns is the right and left cross. The ends go down, one shallow, one deep, and cross to the opposite sides of the field, about a forty-five degree angle. That way the quarterback or the tailback can pass it. It's an option and the ends try to confuse the safety and deep secondary."

Jon assumed his stance. He pulled his arm up to block an imaginary defensive end that could use his hands to knock Jon out of his rhythm and throw his pass-pattern off balance, and was off like a shot. About twenty yards downfield, he abruptly cut across toward the opposite side of the field. Gazali floated in the backfield, allowing his backs to block for him, and sailed a spiral into Jon's waiting arms as he streaked into the end zone. It was hot and they were sweaty.

Jon was about to suggest they call it a day when a strange thing happened. About a hundred and fifty yards away, in the middle of the baseball diamond that doubled as a route for gym classes to run the cross country, they saw for less than thirty seconds a saucer-shaped unidentified flying object land. What attracted their attention were several lights on this saucer. It made no sound. It paused then veered off into the distant north.

"You see that?" asked Jon.

"Yeah. Yes. I did."

"I didn't hear anything. Did you?"

"No. Only dust that rose up when it landed and when it took off," commented Gazali almost in a whisper.

"Lights and dust. Me too."

"If I had seen it, I would not have believed it. But both of us saw it."

They looked over at the houses that lined the cross country route and saw some people standing by their fences and talking with their neighbors. Apparently they also had seen this object land and take off.

"Let's go get some pizza," suggested Jon. "We can talk about this later." As they rode, they occasionally looked at each other with a strange, puzzled look. Jon would shake his head now and then as they pedaled along; Gazali's eyes were like wild eyes.

Once at Gazali's house, they went through the breezeway to the kitchen. The aroma of food, especially pizza, was delicious. Jon's mouth was watering at the same time that he was anxious to convey to Dawn what they had seen at Ridgeview.

"Are you sure that's what you saw?" she asked.

"Both of us saw it," affirmed Gazali.

"You sure it was really there? And not just that you were tired and not having your imagination playing tricks on you?"

"Both of us saw it," Gazali repeated. Jon nodded in agreement. For just this moment his focus was not on the pizza casserole that was cooling in a long dish on the dining room table.

"How long was it there?"

"Maybe a minute," suggested Jon.

"A flying saucer."

"That's right. I know what I saw," repeated Gazali.

"Okay. In the meantime, why don't you have some salad and pizza. It came out of the oven about an hour ago."

They got their plates and put on at least two big slices on them and a token amount of salad since pizza was their main interest. Later that evening when they had polished off about half of the casserole, their conversation returned to the saucer even after Gazali's dad had come in from the yard, having fed the birds and watered the tomatoes, squash, and corn.

Like Dawn, Conrad was skeptical of such things as flying saucers but he had the patience to hear both boys out.

Their credibility was strengthened when the town newspaper, the *Wappo Canyon Times*, ran a whole article on the sighting of this flying saucer. It also published eyewitness accounts, including one off-duty security guard who was playing poker with the some friends when he went to get some more drinks looked out his kitchen window and could not believe what he saw. He called to his poker buddies, even the one who called himself Tahoe Joe, to the window. They too were astonished at what they saw. These witnesses were also interviewed by the crew from station KEGR-TV. It was quite the news item of the month. Reaction to these accounts understandably ran the gamut from complete agreement and belief in unidentified flying objects to skepticism by those who said such sightings were mere optical illusions from overheated imaginations or experimental aircraft from the nearby air force base. Although a local university sent its scientists and astronomers to investigate the landing sight, the area had already been cordoned off by the air force whose own scientists were on site to do the investigating. The university scientists were not invited to participate in the investigation; they simply returned to the university and wrote about it based on eyewitness accounts.

As the weeks passed and football season loomed ahead, the flying saucer landing began to no longer be central in the public mind, especially after the military announced its investigation would take a long time to conduct.

Though they would never forget the flying saucer landing, the football season was fast approaching. Even during the lazy summer days the air had yet a hint of autumn winds to come. Gently would the gold and orange and red leaves almost imperceptibly begin to fall.

The stadium would echo the past amid cheers of the faithful. Pompon girls would twirl with their Ridgeview scarlet and gray pompons. Rebel cheerleaders would create ripples of enthusiasm, cheering, and screaming. Confetti would float after each rebel touchdown. Excitement. Anticipation. The kickoff.

Like generational seasons before them, their days had arrived. It was only a little step. But they were growing up. Sore muscles, aching tendons, pulled hamstrings, and bandaged hands would accompany the glory moments and trench warfare between linemen. Obscurity, even anonymity, in a small town could not lower their eyes from the gridiron greats they so admired. Not just Pop Warner and Jim Thorpe of the Carlisle Indian School. With each pass was a hint of possible greatness. With each devoutly done pass pattern, end run or tailback up the middle, there was desire, inspired by their favorite football immortals: Ernie Nevers and Frankie Albert of Stanford, Johnny Mack Brown of Alabama, Red Grange of Illinois, Rockne and The Four Horsemen of Notre Dame. The list went on and on.

Football was a ritual, as is soccer in many parts of the world, with its own lessons, its own insights. And Jon and Gazali, during their long hot summer and strawberry ice cream days, without having to put it in words, already knew it.

The Hunt

When blackbirds began to eat the cherries on the cherry tree and the peaches on the peach tree or those that had already fallen to the ground, it was obvious no one would buy such a damaged crop. So that morning his father had instructed him to kill all the blackbirds that he could find with a pellet gun he had bought from the Caymus gun shop in town.

The birds had swooped down upon the long gold cat enough; his father had said to protect their nest up in the evergreen tree. And besides, the gold cat was more than hungry, its stomach lean from little food in the past few weeks.

So he loaded the rifle carefully and set out along the tall eucalyptus trees that bordered the dirt road next to their place, their branches swaying with the wind that filtered through the leaves.

The shrill screech of the blackbirds kept them clear in his head from the sparrows and jays and robins that fed in the same place. He saw one perched upon a bare branch that swayed; he aimed, fired and saw it sit there still. He cocked the rifle. Again he fired. This time it swooped limp to the ground, its wings vibrating and hurt.

The gold cat bounded over to it, clamping it between its sharp pointed teeth and running off. He cocked it again and squinted into the leaning eucalyptus leaves that seemed to be hanging fingers of shining ice in the sun's reflection. He saw one that had caught on to the game and quickly flew lazily over him. He shot and missed. The bird flew back among the waving branches and he shot into them, still missing at each firing. He then hid under a canopy that offered him not only shade but camouflage. He waited intently, listening to each shrill cry of the bird that had just eluded him.

He heard the cry and he crept out slowly, keeping as close as he could to the shrubs surrounding the canopy. The black profile of the bird sat squarely facing him and he raised the gun to his shoulder. He shot and missed again.

Again the bird flew over him as if to make him lose shots as the bird knew he could not hit him in flight. He was not that experienced of a hunter. By this time, the cat, its stomach obviously full, emerged from a nearby bush, licking its muzzle as if awaiting another meal, licking its paws and washing its face.

He wanted this bird more with each passing moment, but it flew over him again and again. The cat would love this one for dinner, he thought. But every time he shot, he missed and the bullets flew off into space. The bird knew. He knew. He got six others that day but not the one he wanted.

That evening, after it became too dark to see, he heard the one, the one he wanted, screeching proudly into the sky. He turned on his lamp and read *Field and Stream* until midnight, then turned out the light and rolled over and slept soundly. The morning flooded its light into the venetian blinds of his window. He got up, had bacon, pancakes and eggs for breakfast, and began the morning hunt, peering high into the tree tops. It saw him and screeched twice then flew out over him, repeating what he had done the day before.

He could hear his father drive up the long gravel driveway to the house. He was home early. The rifle shot cracked out, echoing long and almost silent, waving across the sky and echoing against the tree trunks. The proud bird flew across the clouds as backdrop, pausing and swooping, then flapping its wings furiously, soaring like an eagle, lighting into the top branches of a squatty green oak.

He crept up slowly, ever slowly and pointed the barrel through a break in the shrub. The rifle shot cracked the air as he squeezed the trigger; the bird got away, streaking across the pink horizon like an arrow, its streamlined body aiming for the protective eucalyptus branches.

The door closed just loud enough for him to hear; the gold cat rested on its haunches in the bushes, the long dangling leaves tickling its ear, lazily. His father approached with a grey coat with buttoned sleeves, his thin light mustache closely cut.

"How many today?" he asked the boy.

"Four."

"Four?" he exclaimed. The boy turned around.

"Why, yes. I know it's not as many as yesterday but..."

"That's all right, son. The day isn't over yet," he said gazing up at the sun. Then he continued. "You ever get the one you wanted?" The boy shook his head, seeming disappointed in himself.

"Keep shootin' you're bound to get him. If you don't you'll hit one of those stars," he said chuckling.

"The stars don't come out in the day, do they?"

"Probably. But you can only see 'em at night," he said, trudging up the hill to feed the chickens. The boy returned to the shrubbery and in the twinkling of an eye, one of the birds landed on a long telephone wire, sitting there with its wing spread. He aimed and fired. The blackbird fell to the ground, its wings crushed and minute pink blobs of blood like still eyes appeared on the wing. The gold cat dashed to the scene, pawing it and playing with the injured bird.

This time, however, the cat did not wish to eat the bird; he only played with it. The boy could not understand; the cat had always eaten the birds he'd killed before. Why was this one different?

Almost like a reading of the minds, his father came down the hill and paused behind him.

"What's wrong?" he asked his son.

"The cat, he won't eat that bird I just shot for him."

"Well, you know he's probably full. Cats are like people, they can only eat so much. Besides, he may prefer filet mignon at this point," he said eyeing the boy, standing with his gun pointed down.

"I guesso," said the boy demurely. "He's already had four; I guess I can't expect him to eat too many, huh?" His father shook his head and said no. The night fell as quickly as the morning had risen.

The next day was spent doing the chores and shooting intermittently at the blackbirds. He got nine but not the one that continually hovered over him, each and every day until monotony set in and he almost went crazy so strong was his desire to kill the bird. Soon he had, with his faithful rifle, killed over forty birds until there was only the one left, the proud one. The boy became ever so blood thirsty; he wanted that last one, the most prized one, so badly.

Its shrill call sent him flying out the kitchen door to load his rifle and see where the bird was in the tree. He saw it, aimed, and tried to pull the trigger but could not; he was breathing too hard and the sight kept wavering back and forth without aiming straight for the blackbird. Meanwhile the bird perched on a bare set of limbs that thrust out into the dying sun, tossing gently with the wind, making the shrill call to him. He steadied the rifle again, pressing it to his shoulder, confident he would get it this time. No. The sight kept wavering, but again he shot and missed. Enraged, his face turning scarlet from his failures, he ran after the bird firing wildly into the eucalyptus branches, screaming and swearing at the top of his lungs. The bird calmly flew over him, floating on the air then flapping wildly its wings and soaring back into the oak for a moment's perch.

The door slammed and his father emerged, walking toward him, moving in a fast pace.

"What's wrong now?" he said.

"Oh, oh," was all the boy could say.

"Couldn't get him?" The boy shook his head.

"You can't get all of 'em, even though you think you can, son. Come on in and sit down."

The boy walked into a large garage-like room with stuffed pheasants, owls, and deer heads, their eyes peering out in silence as an example of the suffering animals endure unfelt by their sporting human predators. They sat down on the sofas that faced one another. Through the large window, they could see the slanted hills, the green valleys, the hanging trees with the sunlight dancing among the leaves as if in ballet, the marshy meadows with butterflies flitting across them, their wings batting the air.

"I've got every last one of them except that one," the boy began, laying his rifle on the side panel made of knotty pine. His father said nothing for the moment but took down a slender book with the name of Hugo on it in red letters.

"So that's the one you want, huh? The one you been after all this time," he said to the boy as he opened the book, licking his fingers to flip the pages.

"Yes, he's the last one. The last one and then there'll be no more blackbirds to eat the cherries and peaches. His father faintly smiled, still turning the pages. He stopped and scanned the page and read to the boy: "'The teeth can look, just as the eye can bite,'" he said, peering over his glasses at his son. The boy made no response. He just sat there wondering all the while.

"You can't get this one, huh?"

"Not yet." Then after a pause:

"You think you'll get him?"

"Maybe. Maybe if I try hard enough," he said, half-assured.

"Maybe," agreed his father. "Member the other day when I said you may just hit one of those stars?" The boy nodded.

"Well, there's a time you can hit 'em and a time when you can't. Just depends on when you shoot and how you go about it. There's a time for this bird and all the birds that follow. You see, son, you may not hit this one; and you think there's won't be anymore? No, no, no. There'll be more. Tomorrow."

The boy nodded vaguely, his eyes going up to the owl overhead and back down to his father.

"I guesso," he said, agreeing with him. The boy understood, but he never could kill the proud bird. Every day it flew over him, its wings ceasing in mid-flight as if to taunt him and always soaring back into the eucalyptus branches. The bird's call came to his ears but nothing could be done and secretly he was glad.

Music City Skyline

After years of reading it in English, I wanted to learn Chinese so I could translate the *Tao Te Ching* of Lao Tzu. Being a lover of nature, I grew to love the gentle ways of the "Old Master" Lao Tzu who had written this little lovely book of five hundred characters during the Chou Dynasty. So I enrolled in a course in Chinese at Vanderbilt University. It was taught by a professor named Dr. Bo Hamilton. There were eighteen students in the class, including me, most of which were not Chinese. There was Brad Southwell from Lithonia, Georgia who was a political science graduate student from Georgia Southern and who was working on a master's degree in public administration. Another was Gweneth Yuen from Alpena, Michigan, who was also a graduate student in library science; she had finished a degree in humanities and religious studies at the University of Vermont in Burlington. Abra Kapoor was a sophomore English and philosophy major from Manchester, Tennessee. Scott Harrell was a health science and sociology major from Napa, California. We formed a small circle just by sitting next to each other in Dr. Hamilton's class. In the days and weeks that followed, we got to know each other pretty well since we had to go to the language lab to review each chapter in our book of Chinese grammar. It was not only hearing the language of each character that was a challenge. Unlike an alphabet-based language, Chinese was totally different. One stroke of a character could mean a totally different word. In addition, this language basically had four tones: high, low, rising, and falling. Another feature that stood out about this language was it was monosyllabic, not polysyllabic like so many other languages are. And it was how it was said and in what context it was said. Some words were combinations of characters such as dungsyi (which is a combination of east and west) meaning everything, all that there is.

One day as Scott and Abra were coming out of the language lab, Gweneth and I who were headed in their direction, stopped to say hello. In addition, she mentioned there was an eight week class in Chinese calligraphy which was to start the following Monday.

"Yes, let's take it," said Scott.

"Let me see if I can do it, given my schedule," replied Abra. Gweneth and I had already signed up. They needed at least ten students for the class to go. Gweneth mentioned she would call Brad and anyone else she knew that might be interested. As it turned out, we found the ten students needed and the class was a success, given that it was the first time it was offered. It was taught by Mrs. Li Sun who worked closely with Dr. Hamilton and the rest of the staff. They both advocated the importance of Chinese and Asian culture generally since Korean and Japanese were also taught as part of an overall educational experience.

As the days and weeks went by, Scott and Abra often went to the language lab together. After an hour of listening to tapes of vocabulary and conversations in Chinese, they would have lunch together. One day while eating some grits and finishing her slice of pecan pie, Abra asked Scott who had finished his lunch of steamed veggies and cornbread, if he liked the new course in calligraphy.

"I love it," he replied. "I did not know it was so intricate with each character telling a story in the word itself."

"Isn't that something," commented Abra. "It shows how language mirrors a people's history. I like Mrs. Sun too. She obviously loves what she does and how each character has a story."

I, too, came in that day to the Kegger Shack. I had learned to really enjoy steamed veggies and cornbread and an ice-cold soda. Invited to sit with them, we talked briefly about a family visit by Abra's folks the next weekend. But the real focus of our conversation was Mrs. Sun's course. We all agreed that the characters we were learning had more than just conveying information to say. The story and history of the Chinese people were truly amazing. I thought this was fascinating: the character of a country is formed by realizing that among humans each person had to defend his own land with weapons in a well-defined boundary. That's the character pronounced gwō with a long ō. In addition, since China, like many countries or civilizations, assumed they were the center of the world, a kind of ethnocentrism, they were called the middle kingdom. The character for middle was simply a small rectangle lengthwise and to emphasize its being the middle kingdom, a vertical stroke right down the middle emphasized the middle kingdom pronounced jūng with a long ū. So the word for China became Jūnggwō.

中國

As the days went by, Gweneth and I noticed that a romance was beginning to blossom between Scott and Abra; soon Brad, who always seemed to be busy with government and policy concerns, began to notice as well. It was not a situation that was all that demonstrative in terms of love; they were not kissing or hugging, at least not publicly, but it was just a quiet flowing together not just in the language lab but you could see them together in the library, having lunch together, walking across campus together; it was like the red bud trees were secretly already in bloom.

The following week I spent seven hours in the language lab, repeating one sentence after another in Chinese and answering questions based on conversations that were played over and over. Gradually, we all began to recognize characters after having them repeatedly drilled in our heads. It was becoming a language of our own. In our calligraphy class, one of the characters we learned to create by a brush stroke was the character for love. This was so appropriate, especially in light of the romance between Scott and Abra.

The character for love was formed by recognizing that cloudlike vapor rising up from the earth resembles the human breath. Another form of this character looks like three puffs of air breathed into some kind of thing. What gives breath to the heart in a slow, gracious motion is love. For the ancient Chinese, the heart was the seat of the mind since thought as well as feeling develop in the heart. The Chinese character for a heart indicates three beats above a curved hook-shaped character.

As the days and weeks of the semester wore on, the class soon became acquainted with Dr. Hamilton's dog, Sammy who was a terrier-beagle mix and somewhat smaller than a beagle. His nose was more pointed than squared like most beagles and his tail, which had nerve damage when a wind gust blew a door shut when he was a puppy, swung out to the left as he walked or ran. It was not surprising that he understood commands in the four languages in which Dr. Hamilton was particularly fluent, namely Japanese, Chinese, Spanish, and Arabic. He was a smart dog and Dr. Hamilton had him well trained thanks to a stint at obedience school. His diet was the best money could buy, including venison and wild boar, not to mention high protein chicken and beef along with assorted vegetable flavors. The lovely thing about Sammy was his disposition; he was gentle and friendly, not just with grown-ups but with little kids as well as well.

Soon Mrs. Sun introduced the class to a character I was especially interested in, namely the Tao. What on earth did it mean? Isn't that character central in the *Tao Te Ching* (dow-day-jing) by Lao Tzu? Yes, it is. Sometimes the Tao was seen as a metaphysical principle that, when written or spoken, was not or no longer the Tao. "The Tao that can said is not the eternal Tao..."

As a character, Mrs. Sun pointed out that feet running or stopping, in ancient China, meant an "advance," going in a certain way or direction. Then a head with two tufts of hair right on top was how the head was drawn. With the feet and head advancing or going in the same direction, that was the path, the way, or simply called the Tao. So, that was it, the Tao meant your head and your feet were going in the same directions; that was to flow as life flows, to go with the flow, as rivers flow to the sea. The power of that flow stemmed from action that was natural and not forced (wu-wei) and its power, soft like water, could eventually cut through rock.

道

A few weeks later, they had another midterm exam. During the exam, Scott became distracted while he was looking around the room, even at the ceiling, trying to think of the character to fill in the blanks, thus showing he was correctly reading the sentence in Chinese.

Soon his eyes landed on Sammy who was lying on the floor with his paws stretched out before him in a prone position. Scott began whispering to Sammy and this came to Dr. Hamilton's attention. He did not want his dog, however cute and otherwise well-behaved, to become a distraction for his students. Sammy soon looked over at him. Professor Hamilton spoke to him in Chinese: ni dzou ba! This command means: "how about you leave the room." At that point, Sammy got up and went out the door the professor was holding open for him. That did the trick. Students returned their focus to their exams with no further distractions.

Final exams were about two weeks away. They always arrived around the bend faster than any students wanted. But they were coming up. The week prior to finals week, the class was invited to come to Dr. Hamilton's house for the afternoon for a kind of end of the semester party. I drove with Mrs. Sun. Four others decided to ride together in Brad's car, each of them chipping in for some gas money. Brad's car was an old station wagon his folks had given him for his twenty-first birthday. After all, he had achieved good grades at Georgia Southern and had been admitted to Vanderbilt which was considered the "Harvard of the South" for his master's degree.

The day for the party finally arrived. It was an unusually warm, sunny day for December. As they drove up a long driveway, they noticed how upward they were driving so that soon the city was off in the distance below. They came to a driveway that formed a circle around a center garden of beautifully-arranged and well-pruned roses, daffodils, and orchids. A man appeared in a white suit who directed them to a place to park off to one side. Other students from the class were already there since there were five other cars already parked on the same side. Mrs. Sun and I arrived much earlier.

As they moved toward the front door, they could not help but notice a beautiful swimming pool with the water being filtered by a hose that snaked gently back and forth around the pool. On each corner of the pool were statues of what looked like Greek and Roman gods and goddesses. A statue of Zeus, the chief god of the pantheon of divinities on Mount Olympus was on one end. Venus, the goddess of love in the ancient Roman religion, stood at another end. A statue of Athena, the Greek goddess of wisdom, art, commerce and war, stood at another end. And finally, the Greek god Apollo, god of music, poetry, and medicine, stood at the other end.

Another man in a white suit opened the front door and invited us in. They were amazed at an exquisitely beautiful interior with prints in frames from some of the master artists of world art. Over the fireplace was a picture of "Le Moulin de la Galette" by the Impressionist Auguste Renoir. Next to a set of book shelves was a picture titled "A Sunday Afternoon on the Island of La Grande Jatte" by the Post-Impressionist Georges Seurat. Mrs. Sun was already there gazing at the lovely paintings. Soon Dr. Hamilton's wife, Edith, came out to meet the students as did his nineteen year old daughter Mulan. In the next room was a familiar face, namely Sammy who was sprawled on a deep red rug. The dining room had a variety of foods on it, namely everything from pepperoni, sausage, olive, Hawaiian pineapple, and Canadian bacon combination pizza to Chinese food such as broccoli beef, barbecue chicken chow mein, to sweet and sour pork and to sandwich ingredients such as roast beef, cheese, and finally to garlic bread and San Francisco sourdough bread. A variety of soft drinks, sparkling water, and pure mountain water was served by the man in the white suit on a silver platter as he circled among the students who were, not surprisingly, invariably hungry. Students could eat inside the home or sit out on a patio and soak up the sun. As they ate and talked, they could not help but notice a long building that extended along the property. Maybe it was Brad or possibly Scott who asked Dr. Hamilton what it was. He went over and pressed a button just inside the front door to the house. Doors to each rose, revealing cars in each garage. Brad was quite curious; it turned out to be a seven car garage. And these were not any ordinary cars. It turned out Dr. Hamilton was a passionate fan of antique cars. Brad got up and went to the first garage. It turns out Brad was also a fan of antique cars from Rolls Royces to Bentleys.

"And what is this," he asked Dr. Hamilton, pointing to the first garage.

"A 1949 MG," said Dr. Hamilton proudly.

"I like the blue color," commented Brad. Soon Scott and Abra came over. They too were impressed.

"Wow, a Duesenberg!" exclaimed Brad. "My parents used to talk about that one!"

"Yes, that's a 1937 model," commented Dr. Hamilton.

"I sure like the Corvette. I wouldn't mind driving that around," remarked Scott as he smiled at Abra who also seemed tantalized by the 1967 red convertible.

"And this one?" I asked.

"A 1966 Ferrari," commented Dr. Hamilton proudly. "In my dreams I'd love to drive it in the Daytona 500." Brad just smiled as did Scott and Abra.

"But the one I drive the most is the least expensive to drive, this 2003 Honda Accord."

"I would imagine it would cost a lot to drive these others, especially the Kissel Gold Bug Speedster. But you would have to take them out for a spin just to make sure they're in good running condition."

"Exactly. Exactly," said Dr. Hamilton, acknowledging the limits of owning antique cars.

"That's quite a collection," remarked Brad. "Exquisite."

"Thank you, Brad. I have to agree," said Dr. Hamilton, "it's a love I have had for a long time."

"Understandably. As have I...I sure can understand that."

Not long after the shadows began to get longer as sunset approached and it was time for the party to be over. Everyone bid thanks and goodbye to Dr. Hamilton and his family. It had been quite an adventure and an eye-opening one at that. As Brad, Gweneth, Scott and Abra drove down the long, winding driveway so that the lights of Nashville began to outline the city and its prominent buildings such as the Grand Ole Opry, the Capital building and the stadium where the Tennessee Titans play their games, their thoughts turned to what they had seen at Dr. Hamilton's home.

"Could you believe that place?" asked Scott.

"I saw it with my own eyes," said Abra.

"At first I thought Vanderbilt must pay extremely well," commented Brad.

"When I went inside to get some more food, I got to talking with Mrs. Sun and I point blank asked her what about all this luxury. I turns out that Dr. Hamilton is an heir to a lumber and paper fortune," said Gweneth.

"No wonder," said Scott.

"Yet, if he's that rich, why would he go to school to earn a doctorate when he could have spent his days by the pool drinking hot toddies and sipping mint juleps."

"I respect him for that," said Brad. "You're right he could have done that and simply enjoyed his wealth."

"Yet," according to Mrs. Sun, "he went to Vanderbilt, Princeton, and earned his doctorate at Stanford and studied all these languages."

"That's quite impressive. I respect him for that," repeated Brad.

The students came back the following week and took their exams, having temporarily forgotten all they had experienced at Dr. Hamilton's home. Yet I did not. It was a memory of that I will keep for as long as I live. By the way, I found translating the *Tao Te Ching* to be quite a challenge, even after three years of studying the language. Parts of it were straight forward and somewhat easy to literally translate. Then there were other parts of it that lost me. It was very much like venturing into a thicket in which one can get lost. From other translations and even transliterations, the *Tao Te Ching* is a formidable undertaking regardless of how clear a translator tries to make it.

Lifeguard

Lake Hennessey was not the most beautiful lake in the world, but it sufficed. Like most lakes, it was bluish and when winds blew the waters danced on top. Rafael Rountree had been hired as a lifeguard for the summer. It was a needed vacation from his studies as a divinity student. Mr. Bax had hired him on condition that he would work for the entire summer. Ha! Rafael had dreams from the start that he would be taking a long vacation either in Guadalajara with some college friends or a trip to Bermuda with his uncle who lived not far from Galveston.

Rafael's boss was a tall, wiry man in his early forties. He had brown hair with streaks of grey giving him a bleak anemic appearance. Long ears and a country boy charm were his distinguishing features. Often he used the phrase "cotton-pickin'" in his conversations with anybody and everybody. When Rafael first introduced himself, he gave the old country boy smile and stretched his legs the length of the office which stood near the main entrance to the picnic and swimming areas of the lake. Tattoos on both arms could be plainly seen when his sleeves were rolled up on the hot days of this California summer. He introduced Rafael to Satan, his Doberman Pincher, who in emergencies, including illegal deer hunters, was a big help to him. Satan had been trained as a superb attack dog by the local police department.

The place was not only inadequately supplied with only one lifeguard, but in that capacity Rafael was even less fortified with the necessities of life around the lake: a ring buoy, a long pole, etc. Work began in Mid-May and Rafael soon came to the gradual realization that, as much as he needed a better car to drive to school, he did not particularly like this job. He did not project the conventional lifeguard image of a he-man who is ever ready to show off his muscular physique, even though he had been a jujitsu practitioner of several years. Instead he was slightly over two hundred pounds, not particularly muscular, with a shy aggressiveness toward women. His smile could attract women, but as they came closer a sense of doubt clouded their feminine minds and they walked tenderly around him. Descended from a long line of Virginia families, Rafael Rountree, was a burgeoning intellectual with a love for the arts in general and literature in particular. It was, indeed, a poetic nature with an individual philosophy much influenced by the religious and practical philosophy of William James, Josiah Royce, and the theology of St. Augustine. Women usually saw him flash his smile and became infatuated. He drove an older car that fed his need for security, a car he could use to commute back and forth to work. But he wanted a better one that appealed more to women. Rather shy at first, but once you got to know him, Rafael would treat you like one of the family.

Rafael's was a vision in somewhat unreal terms; he could not stand to be scorned or chided by his fellow cohorts. He was extremely sensitive to the everyday shocks and disappointments which often occurred. His humorous side was always welcomed, but his serious side was frankly self-degrading and morose. He had the soul of a poet. He always associated religion and poetry. The two just went together.

As a lifeguard, Rafael lacked only experience which he soon found. But his unreal world would always peep in as the morning sun glare would shine through venetian blinds in his bedroom at home.

Lifeguarding was a routine that Rafael soon tired of. It started him thinking of a quiet little pond in early September when the leaves turned to a golden tint. His lasting happiness was in secluded tranquility along a river back in France or in a hamlet in Norway. Every day for Rafael was the same thing. He would liberally apply baby oil mixed with mercurochrome for a deep, dark, reddish tan. In addition, people would ask him with a curious kind of innocence: "How deep does it get?" And he would give the often-scripted reply: "Nine feet in the middle away from the steps." When a little child would try to sneak past him to swim on the deep side, he would always have to ask: "Can you swim very well?" Frequently the child would give him an insulting look and return to the shallow side. This went on and on in a seemingly endless cycle.

In a few weeks he began an acquaintance with the rangers who patrolled the lake shore in surplus navy jeeps painted a deep forest green. The ranger who helped Rafael the most had, as you may have already guessed, a sense of humor which appealed to Rafael's lighter side. They would sit in Paco's parked jeep deep in chit chat. Paco was in his late twenties and with such good looks he more often than not dated older girls that seemed attracted to him. He was married to a girl originally from Tennessee but who had early moved to Chicago where Paco had met her. "Me and a few friends got drunker than hell one night," continued Paco, "and we was all stoned on our asses and my gal was sittin' the row in front of us. Well, we offered the girls some beer and they took it and soon we were all gassed." "Then what happened? Did you start dating her" inquired Rafael quite curious about the whole affair. "Shore," was Paco's high-pitched reply in Chicagoan tones. Paco's favorite food was Butterfish from the Nappo Fish Market which he dearly loved steamed or pan-fried.

But as the summer progressed, Paco was assigned to patrol the lake shore and the thousand acres in the surrounding area where no deer hunting was allowed. The chats with Paco disappeared in the distance of time and only occasionally was there time enough for a get together. Another ranger was as short stocky big bellied Mexican by the name of Sam who always had a cigar jutting from his mouth. He must have been an admirer of Churchill: all he needed was to have made a "V" sign with his first two fingers. Sam was an understanding sort of person with a nasty laugh that rang out behind his cigar-like turret. His thoughts were not always the most moral, nor were his actions. But as a companion to Rafael, Sam was sure a reliever whenever a broad smile was needed after some baser joke.

Another ranger was Gulstan who was in his last year at Stanford. He was a quiet person and was a picture of human emotional struggle for self-expression. His emotions seemed bottled up inside all ready to explode on some poor unsuspecting bystander. But he also wished to appear older than he was so he would be on an equal footing with the other rangers.

Rafael's most frustrating person among the rangers was Clay. One morning when Rafael drove to the office to pick up the first aid kit and lifeguard sign, one of the jeeps drove up carelessly behind Rafael's car as Rafael was trying to back out of the driveway. In the rearview mirror Rafael saw someone get out, but did not see him clearly. Later Rafael found out what happened. A jeep pulled up to near where Rafael was watching the lake and motioned with his finger to come over. Rafael did and was verbally attacked by Clay's unkind remarks. "Hey buddy, you know you damn near killed me?"

"No sir," came the respectful reply.

"Well you did. Why didn't you stop when you saw me get out?"

"I didn't see you get out," said Rafael, frustrated and embarrassed for many curious people were observing the spectacle.

"Well let me tell you something," continued Clay in threatening tones, "if you do anything like that again, friend, I'll scrub you all over this place."

The last few words rang in Rafael's ears; his sensitive side had been punctured and he felt cut down and held up to ridicule all in one big session. As the day progressed, he felt a simmering anger and resentment toward Clay.

During the weeks that followed, Rafael made sincere efforts at being Clay's friend but it was to no avail. Clay was, as some local girls said, a "real cute guy" but the only problem was Clay knew it. He was self-consciously stuck on himself. He was a conceited ass with little or no feelings for others, not even his wife. Clay's whole world was himself as the measure of all that was valuable. Clay was a living example of what Oscar Wilde once said: "To love oneself is the beginning of a life-long romance."

Clay had been brought up in rough city not too far from his present home. Originally from Indiana, Clay remained aloof and a stranger, mastering the art of holding people off. Rafael found it hard to ask him too many questions because Clay's cockiness and wise remarks instantly poured from his lips. He did not wish to have friends and he hated his job. He once said: "Only a first-rate moron would ever keep this damn job!"

Rafael continued to be bored at his job so he began taking books to work with him since usually an hour or so passed before anyone showed up to picnic or go swimming. He began reading *East of Eden* but never finished it. Poetry was his favorite reading and usually it was short. His favorite poets were Poe, Longfellow, Tennyson, Dickinson, Burns and the Romantics with Keats especially highlighted. Rafael was in love with the lines from the Fitzgerald translation of the "Rubaiyat" of Omar Khayyam:

> "Ah, love, could you and I with Him conspire
> To grasp this sorry scheme of things entire;
> Would we not shatter it to bits
> And remold it nearer the heart's desire!"

Rafael's conflict was inevitable. While wishing the world changed to his heart's desire, he knew full well the wisdom of reformer Voltaire's words: "We shall leave the world as wicked and foolish as we found it."

On weekends a whole new set of rangers would go on patrol because weekends were sometimes marred by the presence of teenage gangs looking for some sort of excitement such as destroying property, snatching purses, staring a riot or give the good ole lifeguard a day of hell. The highlight of the summer season was to be the 4th of July weekend. The civil rights bill in Congress had undergone many long weeks of debate and was finally passed and signed by the Texan President Lyndon Johnson on July 2. The whole ranger outfit knew that black Americans would be out in great number, sometimes sympathetic to the agenda of the teenage gangs.

The morning of July 4 was overcast from fog having disseminated north from the San Francisco Bay Area, but the sun was desperately trying to penetrate the thick misty air. People had, as had been supposed turned out in vast numbers all waiting to celebrate the festivities involved in our nation's most cherished birthday holiday. As Rafael drove north to the lake, he observed all the cars full of people and black Americans had indeed turned out in vast numbers.

Most of the people had come that day for relaxation and enjoyment of the warm California summer. There were over two hundred blacks. While others enjoyed the holiday, one group of black Americans, like some of the gangs mentioned previously, was looking for trouble. Rafael had told a young man whose name was Dan he could drive his car down to the other end of the lake to pick up the picnic equipment of Dan's family. A group of blacks with one muscular one in particular named Rad milled about the corner around which Dan was to drive his car. As Dan began to turn, Rad shoved his leg into the car thus giving cause to bawl out Dan. Rad ripped Dan's car open and shouted: "Hey bud, you almost took my leg off!" Dan was so frightened by this he could not speak. The rangers Clay, Gulstan, and Sam with guns on hips made a quick dash over to the scene. Gulstan made the first attempt at calming Rad down, but Rad replied in belligerent and sarcastic terms: "You's the law in Napa, but I's the law in Vallejo." With his billy club, Clay sent a blow to Rad's biceps. Gulstan had told Rad to take his hands off Dan but he did not immediately do so. Dan then shut his car door and drove to the other end of the lake to pick up his gear. Rad's group shoved the blame on Dan's careless driving, but the rangers had witnessed the whole thing. Rad sat on the part where sand and parking lot pavement met. Rafael had been about thirty feet away, but had not seen the original incident. It is a wonder a riot had not broken out. Rad and his group called it police brutality, especially after Mr. Bax and Satan arrived in a jeep and Rad was soon booked for disturbing the peace.

Most blacks quietly celebrated the fourth and long overdue civil rights, such as stronger right to vote protections and outlawed discrimination in public accommodations, embodied in the bill passed by Congress and signed into law by the President.

From that time on, routine returned. "Can you swim very well?" A head would either nod or shake and that would end it. He had met some colorful people such as Ena Yu who repeated the same phrase every day: "You betta believe it." Rafael suggested he broaden his vocabulary. After all, someone could say "Ena Yu is a fool!" Rafael said: "Are you gonna say what you usually say? 'You betta believe it'"? And to Rafael's frustration, Ena would say "you betta believe it" anyway.

Then there was an eleven year old girl who was rather pudgy who would wear a bikini and come by and say: "Hi, Mr. Lifeguard." She would then try to tell Rafael how others were always mistreating her and calling her "fatso" or a "whale in a bikini." As a public servant, Rafael realized you cannot solve everyone's problems to their perfect satisfaction.

By this time, in late August, he was looking forward to the classes he would be taking during the next school year such as The Jews: A history of Discrimination, New Testament Theology, Muhammad and the Qur'an, a beginning course in the language that Jesus probably spoke, namely Aramaic, and courses in Mahayana Buddhism, Pastoral Counseling, Hinduism, the Psalms, Religion and Art in America, and Taoism.

He turned in his keys, thanked Mr. Bax and the rangers for their support throughout the summer, and drove off through the vineyards and shaded trees of the Napa Valley. He enjoyed being a lifeguard more than he thought he would and some of the memories would stay with him throughout his life.

Indian Summer's Dream

Thoughts of the finality of his father's death haunted him. He could not manage to cease dwelling upon a loss that was forever. Long August days stretched like arms in an El Greco painting into Indian summer. At night such thoughts so disturbed him that once he even was afraid to go to sleep for fear he would never wake again, that he, too, would be gone. Forever.

It had been weeks since he had seen his father's face. How different Papa looked. How he lay there in the casket. How friends and family solemnly approach it, paused, whispered, and each had imprinted on the retina of the eye their last picture of him. Papa had been dressed in a bluish tweed suit, his dark hands folded on his chest, his wedding band on his finger, all strictly convention. He appeared so different.

At this juncture, where hellos and goodbyes are dawns apart, he was amazed how friends sprung out of the network of their common humanity. People really were kind. It was as though his father's face was their mirror too. Pallbearer Bill Templeton said: "I've lost a part of me." Long-time friend Jim Bosche whispered: "He was the best. We're gonna miss him." There was also so much food. Chicken both grilled and fried, mashed and scalloped potatoes, spinach, steak, garden salads, deviled eggs, sodas, sliced carrots and tomatoes, freshly-perked coffee, and green tea. It was as if when folks died the survivors had to have food lest they grow hungry.

His mother never recovered. Not after thirty-eight years of marriage. It was so hard for her. Everything changed. Her entire world.

He had once dreamed of his parents' deaths. He had awakened with a start. But he realized it was only a dream.

Now he was twenty-eight. Dream had turned into reality. The loss was an abyss, an ever-widening abyss when care was that close was in the game. It was hard to take. Diamond-hard.

His brother, Lamar, did not say much. Maybe he did not know what to say when it came to such transitions. It was better not to even think about such things. You had to love, to continue, he thought.

Martha, his sister, had cared for Papa during the long and agonizing months of his illness. She thus felt the profound sense of loss as well as a deep sense of relief from the rounds of care. She would soon be able to turn her attention back to her husband and daughters.

At their last meeting he and Papa had been strangers. Papa had been understandably irritable. The cancer had spread, first through the inner lining of the left lung. Surgery could have stopped the spread had Papa not already had pneumonia in his right lung. Although the pneumonia eventually cleared, Papa grew more and more isolated. He was so weak, due to weight loss and lack of appetite, the surgery was thought to be no longer an option. Dr. Miksa and his staff had not recommended surgery because it would have made Papa's condition more dangerous. It was just a matter of months even weeks; each day became a death rehearsal. At Papa's request, Dr. Miksa did not hint of the extent of the severity of Papa's illness. The family was thus kept in ignorance. Throughout the long days of early summer Papa could hear the periodic dull thuds of apricot that had ripened and fallen on the ground outside his bedroom window. Zucchini as well ripened in the lazy summer's sun.

His mother did not realize how sick Papa really was. Papa was secretive and stoical about the severity of his condition. Yet his mother felt the distance, the ever-parting waves on the seas that separated them. Finally, in mid-July, he remembered, she had to get away from the pain and the parting. She flew to Tennessee to visit relatives, including a son who was a student in summer school at Vanderbilt.

Even two thousand miles away could not get Papa off his mother's thoughts. She enjoyed the dancing would-be stars at Opryland; the musicians hoping to cut a record and make it big at the various record companies on Music Row and Studio B where Elvis Presley recorded many of his songs; the fascinating history of the Hermitage, the home of President Andrew Jackson; and the serenity and art of the Cheekwood Botanical Gardens. Even the white pillars of

Nashville's Belle Meade Mansion and the statue of Athena, Greek goddess of wisdom, at the Parthenon, a replica of the Parthenon that stood on the Acropolis in ancient Athens, Greece, momentarily captured her attention. At night, however, her thoughts raced from Tennessee to California. Phone calls yielded from Martha a mixture of apprehension and thinly-disguised assurances.

After two weeks, she just had to fly home. She bought Davy Crockett coonskin caps and toys for Martha's girls, said goodbye to her relatives and son, and turned her thoughts homeward bound as Nashville lights disappeared in jet windows. Something told her it was time to resume with Martha the care of Papa. Family support in times of crisis was what made such junctures bearable at all.

When his mother arrived home, joy seemed everywhere, even in Papa's distant face. He even managed a smile at the coonskin caps. He never looked so good. It was as though everything would be better, that tomorrow would bring a sunnier day. A glow, translucent, curiously enough, bathed his face. Even the seventy-three pounds he had lost from chemotherapy in the last six months did not seem to intrude upon the touch of arms who had shared thirty-eight years. Little did his mother suspect.

He remembered how the news came. It was like hang gliding over a ridge of oak-clustered hills, hay-colored in late-July bloom. The call from his sister. Shocked. Broken. Martha, a courage in bones, discovered the blood-streaked sheets. His death had come in the night. It was not like Byron's gallant efforts on behalf of Greek independence; nor was it a death by dismemberment by a serial killer; or death among many other faceless numbers on battlefields such as Gettysburg, Verdun, Pearl Harbor, the Somme, Gallipoli, Wounded Knee Creek, Sluys, or The Bulge. It was not that conventional. His death was quiet and at home, not hospital centered. His death simply came: the metastasizing cancer cells had severed blood vessels in the lung and hemorrhaging resulted. Small blood puddles lay near the bed where he had tried to cough away the air-drowning blood.

Even as Martha called an ambulance, the mid-morning heat quivered from the asphalt of Foster Road and the already reddish color on the Santa Rosa plums his father had

81

grafted in the spring deepened. The ambulance siren seemed somehow muted. The heat on this last July day seemed to muffle drums of passing blood and bone. All other concerns now seemed trivial, even petty. Even nightly denials by the President concerning alleged knowledge of the Watergate break-in slipped into irrelevance. Death trivializes our petty graspings, he thought.

Martha was strong. Her grief was not brief; it would extend for years. She alone would visit his grave on a regular basis while the rest of the family tried to somehow forget in order to live. The guilt, the resentment, the entire process first had to be cut short due to business considerations. From casket and cemetery selection down to the color of Papa's last suit were considerations that had to be faced. Such were the concerns for a family that faced a death in the family for the first time. His mother was in no shape to make such decisions; her eyes were bloodshot. Martha and her Vanderbilt son who had flown home from Nashville were the ones who made such choices; Lamar, forty miles away, was keeping his mind off the scene from throwing himself ever more fitfully into his family and his work.

Soon the initial shock began to wear off; reality insinuated itself. Never again the laughter, the jokes. So many things he had wished to say to Papa; if only he had said them. Never would they be said. Right now he wanted to talk to him. As weeks passed, however, the earth turned a deeper hay color; the Santa Rosa plums ripened into juicier maroon morsels. Zuchini were picked when tender; the apricots were gathered in time. Amid Indian summer days a hint of autumn was yet in the air. Rivers continued to flow from mountains to the sea.

There was nothing else, he thought. You died and that was it. Yet death was horrible, so personal, so devastating when it touched your life and those for whom you deeply cared. Finality was what hurt. He always tried to view things scientifically. The women at the funeral were sentimental. His mother relied on faith; Martha's strength sprang from not only her faith but her sheer determination to survive. He remembered sitting quietly, almost lost in his own thought, as Reverend Wolter Vanbrugge painted a word picture of a ship receding over the horizon. Death, he said, was a farewell and a time to look life's mysteries in the eyes.

The church organist, Kara Melton, played "Abide With Me" in a dirgeful manner; he remembered comforting his mother and staring at a wreath of red roses next to the open casket. Once the eulogy and the music and the hymns were over, guests filed by the casket to take one last look. That face he would not forget: Papa's face was like clay that had been smoothed. He remembered how sex had become almost an obsession; life could grasp at straws that way. Sex and death were kissing cousins; an affirmation of life no matter what. He had nudged next to the tenuous edges of human finitude.

One evening several weeks later, he was reclining on the screened porchway of the house. A lamp was on but not directly overhead. The rattan chaise lounge was comfortable even though he lay on his right side away from the lamp. The lamp was the only genesis of light. Familiar sounds of crickets and the low, nearly inaudible hum of the television inside the house could be heard. Slowly he slid into a light sleep; in fact he was quite aware of everything at once. He looked over his shoulder. Gradually it dawned on him the leg he saw out of the corner of his eye was the same leg sticking out from under Papa's bed sheet he had seen numerous times during Papa's last days. He did not turn to gaze at the rest of his body. He knew it was Papa; it had to be.

"We're at a loss," he began.

"You needn't be," the voice replied in almost inaudible tones.

"You mean everything is okay?"

"Yes. Very well," came the reply.

"But it's horrible. Mom is taking it the worst," he said in half-awe.

"Everything's all right," came the reply.

"How can you say that?"

"It just is. Just is. No need to worry," came the reply. He peered over his shoulder. The legs were still there, reclining. There was a long silence; the crickets now seemed far in the distance, the light more dim. Then he continued:

"But all the times we could've said. The finality of it."

"There's no need to worry. Believe me. All is well."

At that moment he awoke. He did not say anything to anyone. He was reassured. A wake of calm fan-tailed over him like a warm, turquoise sea. Clutches of finality no longer gripped him. Serenity now massaged his fear, his loss, and his anxiety. A dream, he thought, only a dream. He could have seen a ghost or possibly a reincarnation of his father, but he did not. He only saw his legs. Perhaps waking was only a dream among other dreams. From that night forward, he felt that there was something that did not die, a shadow that somehow remained. He did not know why or even how.

For the first time in weeks he finally slept soundly and deeply. He never slept so well as he did after this dream.

Peace and Quiet

Truman Tokala had had enough of the bustle and hectic push and pull of life in San Francisco. Each day he would look out his fifth story office window and see the people clamor hurriedly across the wide street below when the traffic light would change from red to green. What he needed was rest; a peace and quiet only the wide-open country had ever afforded him.

Two weeks were his according to his thin, white-mustached boss, Edsel Covington, to vacation wherever he desired. Immediately he drove home, packed a suitcase and sleeping bag, and wound his way through the maze of honking horns and near misses and began to drive north to the Valley of the Moon or to the Napa Valley wine country.

He had been there before. The cars began to slightly thin out as he drove in the summer night. Briefly it rained, leaving the air smelling sweet as it often does. Crossing into Sonoma Country, dusk spread over him with a faint glow.

The highway rolled gently over plains and hills that appeared at every turn in the dusk, the stone fences flashing by his window. He spent one day in Glen Ellen, north of Sonoma, visiting the burned out remnants of Jack London's Wolf House.

He then decided the Napa Valley seemed promising so he left soundlessly and stopped near a long eucalyptus lane that formed a dozens of weird shadows along the road. Here, the stars were blocked from view. He parked the car and finding a soft, open spot in a vineyard, bedded down for the night. About midnight, a pair of headlights showed dimly down the road but as they drew nearer and nearer, shining reflection upon the hood of his car that was snugly parked next to a thick eucalyptus trunk. He sat up. The car approached and stopped several yards down. He listened and heard screams. He strained his eyes to see.

"No, no, no. Get away! Get away from me!" came the screams. Truman stood and began walking cautiously in their direction. The headlight suddenly turned on the car and started with a roar, speeding toward him. Frozen and blinded by the glare, he stood solidly. The car, however, just missed him but sent him rolling into a ditch, knocking him out. The car sped away, its gears straining.

Silently came the dawn. Sunshine slanted above him, piercing the branches that swayed with the breeze. He stared upward, gashes on his face, his clothes torn, his hands scratched and slicked with dried blood, his body in much pain. Straining every muscle, he cleared the shallow edge of the ditch and rolled onto the dirt alongside the paved road. There he laid for several hours.

Late afternoon sun shone through the branches on the other side of the road. A car stopped and a fat but tender-faced woman, a Mrs. Gutzborg, fetched a pail of water and some rags, gave him a drink, and washed his face. She helped him into her station wagon and drove him down the road a piece to a ranch stocked with Black Angus cattle and three palomino horses.

"What happened?" she finally asked, pouring him some coffee.

"I just decided to sleep out there. Under the stars. And pretty soon. Pretty soon," he said pausing to press his fingers to his temples, "I saw these headlights coming my way. I heard screams. Then they came after me," he said groggily.

"Who's they?" she asked, sipping her coffee.

"Don't know," he said, shrugging. Her husband, Arvid, came through the screen door and she told him all about it. He shook his head.

"Could've been them car gangs from up valley," he suggested, rubbing his fingers through his grey hair.

"I doubt it," she replied as Truman felt the bandages on his hands and knuckles.

"You're welcome to rest here if you'd like," she offered.

Having declined her offer, he set out to retrieve his car and start on the road north. As he was unlocking his car door, he heard a voice, a faint one, that penetrated the air despite the breeze that now blew. He walked down the road a piece and gazed long into the vineyard basking in the valley sun. The voice groaned harshly and beneath a slender but full-foliaged bush he found the beaten body of a young woman.

He lifted her limp body and carried her to his car and slid her into the front seat. She mumbled a few indistinct words that he could not understand. Torn and ripped clothes and a bruised face were all that characterized her. Behind the grey steering wheel, he sped down to the ranch house.

It took awhile, but Mrs. Gutzborg gradually revived the beaten girl, Jamie Williams. High cheek bones, faintly pink lips, and deep auburn hair highlighted her face. Her lips were high and thin and her child-like demeanor sent a glow that spread all over her.

"How did all this happen?" asked a perplexed Mrs. Gutzborg.

"Well, it all started when I needed a ride to my aunt's house in Sonoma. Father let me off at my girlfriend's house as he had to go to Lake County to visit some friends. I thought I could get a ride from her but she wasn't home. So, I started walking and soon this car came up and two boys inside offered me a ride. I said no thanks, but as the road was deserted at that hour, they got out and dragged me into their car. One of them reared back and socked me; that's all I remember," she said tearfully. Mrs. Gutzborg made her sit back in the lounge chair and rest her head.

"And then they forced you?" concluded Mrs. Gutzborg. Jamie nodded, peering down at herself. Truman sat there and drank his coffee, looking at her in pity, empathetic almost to the point of revenge.

"You know where they were from?" asked Truman.

"Up valley, where I live," she said, pausing to glance out the window. "I'm grateful to you both," she said. "If it hadn't been for you, I'd probably be dead right now." They remained at the ranch for two days and then began the trip north.

As they drove through the valley, the vineyards passing like rows of soldiers, she recounted the story over and over as if once or twice was not enough. Then silence.

"It must be something to be a big business man in San Francisco," she remarked.

"Not as big as you think," he replied perfunctorily.

"Why not?"

"Oh, the story of it fades. You get old and then they bring in new blood," he said as the purple-hooded hills passed slowly, carving a silhouette against the pin-streaked horizon.

"New blood?" He nodded.

"Yeah, the new generation. As if they couldn't propagate them fast enough! Young execs in the firm," he said.

"Where do they come from?" she asked naively.

"The womb. Where else?" At this he chuckled low then added, "colleges and business schools every year, my dear."

"Oh," she said then asked, "Don't you have a wife?"

"No. Never needed one."

"Why not?"

"Why I never needed one? Because I was always too smart for that little game. After the army in Korea, my buddies, all of them ran off and got married. Just plain crazy. I couldn't understand it," he commented, completely oblivious of her. They drove more silent miles alongside a swiftly moving Southern Pacific train rumbling on the tracks next to the highway.

She moved closer to him as the miles sped easily by. A brilliant orange lit up the dip in one of the purple, oak-splotched hills that back dropped seemingly endless rows of grapes.

"I want to thank you for saving me," she said, regarding him strangely.

"You do? Thank you is enough for me."

"No, but I want to give you a thank you to remember," she said, encircling him in her arms and kissing him long next to his mouth.

He gave her an odd look. In minutes they stopped at the Olde Kegger and bought some beer then continued north, the dotted lines becoming darker with each passing mile. She snuggled next to him, warmly. They drank as the tender night hugged them in its arms.

"Why won't you tell me where you live?" he asked quietly.

"Because I want to live with you," she replied, hugging him again.

"Look here," he began.

"No. I want to make that my thank you to you," she insisted. His arguing was of little value for she had made up her mind. They turned off the highway that stretches far into the valley and rented a hotel for the night with separate rooms.

Around eleven o'clock, she knocked on his door. When he opened it, she threw herself at him. To bed they went, bandages and all. Love has a way of removing obstacles, if you can call it love.

Next day, they drove off into the shadows of the looming, moss-strewn oaks that guard the country bridges and came to a pond surrounded by reeds.

"Let's go for a swim," she suggested.

"Forgot my suit. Besides, these bandages might come off."

"So what," she replied. Removing her clothes, she began wading. Truman Tokala, looking for peace and quiet, was not to be outdone. He dashed nude into the pond, exhibiting his fine back stroke, reminiscent of his days on the Cal varsity.

Impressed by such precision, she kissed him. She knew her father would not worry so she remained with Truman for several days. The nude swim put her in high spirits. They stopped at the wineries and endured the hot, muggy summer's day. The valley temperature rose to one hundred and five degrees in the afternoon. They swam again, this time in an unheated pool.

Across the way, a familiar face stood out, a face that frightened her. Emilio Robles stared long at her, studying her with the trained eye of a dog. He got up and left the pool. Truman thought nothing of it but Jamie was afraid. At sunset they climbed in the car and drove off. As they pulled into the driveway of Jamie's home, a green car was parked inside.

Four Mexicans emerged, walking in a line, their hair like sweat in the sun. No one seemed to be home at her house. On they came.

"You give us Jamie, man," said one harshly.

"Why?" snorted Truman.

"Cause we want her," Emilio said. "And we want her now, you hear?"

"Sure," said Truman, "I hear." Tears came to Jamie's eyes. A knife blade showed in Emilio's hand.

"She's my woman, you know," Emilio declared, the others staring at Truman and not blinking an eye. "She's mine."

Truman turned to Jamie.

"Why is he saying that?" She shrugged.

"Look, man, you've been hurt already. Just give us Jamie and we won't bother you no more," said Ramon, his black eyes sparkling.

Jamie ran back to the car while Truman defiantly stood there facing them.

"Obviously she doesn't want to go with you boys so why don't you just leave her alone," he said.

Emilio was the first to lunge at him, hurling his body at Truman like a mountain lion. He fell back against a hedge next to the gravel driveway, blood dripping down his temples.

Ramon grasped Jamie hard about the arms, wrestling with her. Muffled sirens in the background scattered them, leaving Jamie and Truman together with threats and profanity.

The police drove in, crunching the gravel under the tires and got out.

"Boys from around here, eh?" said officer Noriko. Jamie nodded.

"This your home?" Again she nodded.

"Why're they after you?"

She began crying. Emilio slowly walked to them as officer Turi frisked him quickly. At that moment, no knife was on him.

"Why are you after this girl?" said officer Noriko.

"Because she's gonna have my kid," Emilio replied, his black mustache moving with his lips. They all looked at her.

"Your child?" said the surprised officer.

"Si. She found out she was pregnant two weeks ago. I didn't want no kid at first. That's why we beat her. But now..." he said, going silent. She leaned into Emilio's arms, crying.

"You know anything about this?" Truman Tokala shook his head. Since the police had no more questions for him, he got into his car and drove off, maybe, just maybe, to find some peace and quiet. At last.

The Night the Bulldozers Came

"I'm waiting for a bulldozer to crash through my office sometime and clear my desk of papers," Doc Hinto once said. His office was a cubbyhole decorated with modern designs, family portraits, and a desk and telephone. It was off the Stanford campus or you thought so by the time you had passed the radiation lab, the engineering buildings, and the parking lot that resembled a football field.

I don't know what got into me when I awoke at half past twelve one night in late February. I looked around, blinked, and sprang out of bed. Putting on my coat, I dashed down the corridor and out into the crisp, clear night. I had heard the sounds of bulldozers weaving about in my head, like the rattling of thousands of miniature bells, softly clanging until my mind felt as if it would expand out to the edge of the universe and suddenly stop when time reached zero.

Dashing across the Spanish style quadrangle, I saw the face of Christ on the church bathed in iridescent light as purple as the evening. I felt timeless, out of and beyond time. I was nowhere and everywhere at once. What about the Floridian who worked so late? Wasn't he everywhere at once? Doc Hinto was from the "buckle on the Bible belt," Gainesville, Florida. He didn't like it there and I suspect he didn't like it here either.

I crossed Panama Drive, jogged through the half-muddy sidewalks, under the hanging moss that covered the parking lot like a shaggy blanket. Rounding the bend, I saw a light from his office. I ran to the green door, banging my fists on it, kicking it. Then footsteps. He opened the door, his red, pudgy chin-clefted face seeming weary from his writing for New York publishers.

"What's wrong, Mr. B?" he asked in his soft accent.

"What's wrong?" I exclaimed. "The bulldozers are coming that's what's wrong."

"I've heard of Santa Claus coming. But I never..."

"What did you have tonight? Bourbon? Southern Comfort? Hot Toddy? Whiskey Sour? A Dry Martini?" he said, his tone unchanged.

"No, no, no. I'm not drunk, Doc. Honest."

"Come in and take a load off your feet," he said quietly trying to get back to his work. A sheet of paper was tucked in his typewriter as we entered the cubbyhole.

"Now, Mr. B., you know as well as I no bulldozers are coming this way. Besides, even if they were coming, I'd simply go out and salute them. So calm yourself. Would you like some coffee to sober up?"

"I told you. I told you I am not drunk. I tell you I heard the bulldozers coming straight for your office. I honestly did. Now you must know how Georgians felt when they heard General Sherman was cutting through Georgia to the sea."

"How can I feel that way when I'm not a southern sympathizer? What are you trying to do, enter my subscription to Atlanta magazine? Or trying to get my mother's recipe for good old-fashioned Kentucky Mint Juleps? Aha, Mr. B., I think I've got your little game. You mean to tell me you came running all the way over here to make me feel like a Georgian so I'd give you some of the pecan pie my mother sent me in today's mail? Come, come, Mr. B. I just don't believe Georgians felt that way nor do I welcome your trying to gain access to my Pecan Pie or, to say the least, to my Mint Julep recipe while I editorialize in the *Washington Reporter*."

He laughed it off and began staring at the window. Before I knew it, his mouth dropped open as he stared out into the night. A light, pink snow had fallen on the lawn outside and lined up on all sides were bulldozers with their blades aimed right at old Doc. He could not believe it. He turned to me, his face now pale with shock.

"My God, bulldozers *are* out there. At least four or five of them." He looked back at me, his mouth opened wider.

"Each driver, if I'm not mistaken, is one of the students I gave low grades to last quarter. Good God, am I dreaming? Mr. B. do I look all right to you?"

"You do look a little pale, Doc. Didn't I tell you there were bulldozers out there?"

"Yes, but I didn't believe..." He stared out the window again, shaking his head slightly. "Good grief! They're starting their motors. I'd better evacuate. Let me see. Anything I need?" He picked up a stack of the *New Republic* and began to go out the door. He leaned back in.

"Mr. B?"

"Yes, Doc."

"If you can get rid of them, I'll, I'll give you that recipe."

"I don't need your recipe, Doc. I tell you what, why don't you just move your desk out the door and let them shove all these papers off?"

"I don't think they want the desk. They want me, Mr. B. Me." He took off and I followed.

"*Now*, do you know what the Georgians felt like?"

"Yes. I must admit I do. Damn that Sherman anyway. Why does he have to come back and haunt me. I studied him in college, you know."

We passed through the door and out onto the new-fallen snow where the bulldozers were readied. Presently, Doc pulled out his hanky as a symbol of truce.

"One thing about it, Mr. B."

"What's that, Doc?"

"We southerners never seem to finish surrendering, do we?"

"I guess not, Doc." At that moment, he threw up his hands and surrendered.

About the Author

A native of Honolulu, Richard Alan Bunch grew up in the Napa Valley. His poetry works include *Collected Poems 1965-2011*, *South by Southwest*, and *Wading the Russian River*. He is the author of short stories such as "Whipped Cream" and "Hey, Short Stuff!" and the novel *Cornet and Clarinda*. His plays such as *The Russian River Returns* and *A Crude Awakening* have appeared in several venues. His poetry has appeared in *New Contrast, Meridian Anthology, Fire, James River Poetry Review, Wavelength, Green's Magazine, Kinesis, Footprints, Latino Stuff Review, Albatross, Kimera, Twilight Ending, Splizz, Prairie Winds, Carpe Laureate Diem, Brownstone Review, Northwest Florida Review, Tule Review, Pinion, Offerta Speciale, Northern Stars Magazine, Chaffin Journal, Enigma, The Quest, Ruah, Sun Poetic Times, Quantum Leap, Beyond Doggerel, Sepia, Amber, Japanophile, New Mirage Quarterly, Lucid Moon, The Lamp-Post, The Open Bone, Mind in Motion, Takahe, The Lucid Stone, Dirigible, Illya's Honey, Axe Factory Review, European Judaism, Coe Review, Poetry Nottingham, Xavier Review, Red River Review, Cape Rock, Cold Mountain Review, Dan River Anthology* and the *Oregon Review*.

CPSIA information can be obtained at www.ICGtesting.com
Printed in the USA
BVOW01s0202081113

335738BV00006B/90/P

9 780741 498496